PERIPHERAL

DAN MAYER

Black Rose Writing | Texas

This is a work of fiction. Names, characters, businesses, places, events, and incidents are either the products of the author's imagination or used in a fictitious manner. Any resemblance to actual persons, living or dead, or actual events is purely coincidental.

ISBN: 978-1-68433-366-0
PUBLISHED BY BLACK ROSE WRITING
www.blackrosewriting.com

Printed in the United States of America
Suggested Retail Price (SRP) $16.95

Peripheral is printed in Calluna

Thanks to Patricia and Earl for their support in the beginning,
and to Justina and Cora, who read it first.

PERIPHERAL

CHAPTER ONE

Space cadet, fatty and pimples were all charming names from my youth. I prefer Jack.

I'm 29 now, and in the best shape of my life. People from my past would hardly recognize me now.

It's early August and it's still summer holidays for another few weeks. I'm a special education teacher and I like to start the week before, just to make sure I have everything in order, for the start of the new school year.

I'm single, recently single. My girlfriend thought that things were getting too weird for her, and she bailed. I don't blame her. I miss her and I'm sure she misses me too, but she just couldn't handle it anymore.

You're probably wondering what happened between us, and what it was that scared her off. Well, that's what I'm about to explain. I hope to anyway. I still haven't figured all of it out myself yet.

I'll get to that, but first things first, a little bit about me...

I was born August 6th, 1985, to Bill and Irene Armstrong. My Dad is a mechanic and my Mom was a stay at home Mom for about 7 years or so. She started working when my sister went into kindergarten. Now Mom works in a deli downtown. She loves it, because she gets to be around people every day. She is definitely the outgoing one in our family. Dad and I are more reserved than my Mom and my sister falls somewhere in between. From the outside looking in, we seem like an ordinary family.

My sister is a family therapist, specializing in helping people cope with family members experiencing dementia or psychological problems. It's no coincidence that we both chose the fields we are in, given our family history.

Mom and Dad are happily married after 35 years of marriage. They had their tough years, but they stuck it out and now they are happy as can be. We have always been a close family, always spent holidays together, and my parents made sure we were as well rounded as possible.

Helen, that's my sister, is married with two kids. Her husband's name is Jason and I couldn't have asked for a better guy for her. They live just around the block from my parents and just a couple of streets over from me. I guess you could say that we are still a close-knit family. We see each other almost daily and are very involved in each other's lives. I go to almost all my nephews' games, whether it's soccer in the summer, or hockey in the winter.

I've never been married, and I don't have any children. I've always been a little scared to have children, given our family's history. I was a loner for most of my younger life. I didn't start making friends until I got to high school and started to play sports. I was a late bloomer, as they say.

I'm waiting for Jason to finish buying some last-minute things from the grocery store. I'm going to tag along with him, my sister and my nephews on a fishing / camping trip for a few days. It will give my sister and I some much needed time to talk in private, maybe when he and the boys are off fishing. I can tell that she knows there's something up. We are far too close for us to keep secrets from one another. I feel terrible that I've kept my secret as long as I have.

My parents were young and just starting out, when they got pregnant with me. I wasn't planned but I was welcomed nonetheless. They brought me home from the hospital and were thrown into parenthood, unprepared. Both came from small families, so neither of them had been around infants before. That is why my Grandmother came to stay with us. She was my Dad's mom, and she lived with us for nearly six months. I don't remember this of course; I just remember the stories that I have been told.

Grandma, as it turned out, wasn't much help to my parents. They spent as much time looking after her as they did caring for me. Apparently, she developed dementia shortly after moving in with us, or so they thought. She was prone to disappearing for periods of time. Something I can relate to, only recently. Oh, and she had a secret as well.

I remember going to see Grandma in Forest View retirement home, when I got older. One visit in particular stuck in my mind. This was the visit, as it turned out, that shaped my childhood. It kind of scared me then, but I understood more as I got older.

I was 7 at the time. Dad and I went alone, while Mom and Helen stayed home. I don't remember why. I just know that it was Dad and I that visited her on that day.

I remember it like it was yesterday. It was late spring, and the snow had just finished melting. It was warm enough to take her outside for some fresh air and that is exactly what we did. The three of us went down by the small lake on the property. The large expanse of green grass sloped gently down to the edge of the water. The water's edge was lined with cattails everywhere but a little stretch of sand that lie directly in front of three wrought iron and wood benches, that were at the present, vacant. Dad and Grandma sat on a bench and talked, while I fed the ducks some pieces of bread and crackers that we had brought for them. Four of the ducks were mallards and one was a larger white domestic duck. I finished feeding the ducks all that I had, and they slowly moved off. It didn't take long before I was bored and started to throw rocks into the lake. All the rocks were big and round, not suitable for skipping, and so I quickly lost interest with that as well. I sat on Dad's knee and listened to him and Grandma talk. She was having a good day; something that was getting less frequent as the months passed. There were times when we came to visit her, and she didn't recognize us at all. When it first happened, I didn't understand.

"It's me, Jack! How can you not remember me?" I pleaded with her, but she stared through me, as though I wasn't there.

"Why doesn't she remember me, Daddy?"

"Well, Jack. Sometimes as people get older they develop a condition called Alzheimer's or dementia. These are just fancy words for saying that they forget a lot. Sometimes they remember, or they may forget. Usually they forget more and more as time goes on."

"I forget stuff all the time. Does that mean that I have dementia or elvesheimers?"

"No, Jack, it doesn't," Dad said, laughing.

I didn't truly understand until many years later. Anyway, on this particular day, she was completely lucid. We spent most of the afternoon with her. The visits were always long when she was having one of her good days, and rather short when she wasn't. I should say that she was completely lucid at the beginning of the visit, but that all changed.

We had been visiting for a couple of hours and Dad had to run up to the main building to do some adult stuff. He left me with Grandma, since she was having one of the best days I could remember.

"Okay Jack, I have to go up to the office, sign some papers and go to the washroom and I'll be right back," Dad said.

"What should I do if she starts having a bad day?" I whispered.

"She'll be fine, she's having a good day, besides I won't be long," he said, rustling my hair with his hand, before turning and jogging up the gentle slope to the main building.

"I guess it's just you and me kid," Grandma said.

"Yeah, I guess so," I said, sheepishly.

"Come, sit here beside your old Granny. I won't bite, I'll tell you a story," she said, patting the bench beside her.

I hopped up on the bench and sat cross-legged facing her, ready for her story to begin. Grandma was a good storyteller, and she sure didn't disappoint on that day, although it had more to do with her demonstration than the actual story itself.

"When I was a young child, we didn't have all the modern conveniences that you young people have today. No, we had to work hard for everything we had. I think it made us appreciate things more, you know?"

I nodded in agreement, even though I wasn't completely sure what she meant.

"Anyway, I lived on a farm in the country, miles from town. If we wanted to go into town, we had to walk or take a horse, or horse and carriage. So, we really didn't leave the farm all that much. We never had time to get bored; too much to do on the farm. We had our chores to do every day, and when we weren't doing them we were exploring down by the river, when it was warm enough to do so. What I'm about to tell you, I never told your Father. I'm telling you because I can tell that you are like me and my Father, and my brother. It runs in families, you know.

Anyway, one day after I finished my chores early, I went down to the river to go fishing with my brother. When we got there my Dad was standing on the bank of the river with his back to us. We couldn't see what he was doing, so my brother and I stopped to watch from a distance. We didn't want him to see us for fear of him giving us more work to do. He didn't hear us approach, because the sound of the river drowned out all but the loudest of noises. There were a good set of rapids in the middle part of the farm and they could be quite loud when the water was high, as it was on that day.

"Before I continue, I have to ask. Do you know what peripheral vision is, Jack?"

"I'm not sure Grandma, I've heard it before, but I guess I don't," I said.

"That's okay, I'll explain it to you, and then I'll continue with my story," she said, pausing to change position on the bench.

"Peripheral vision is, what you can see sideways, when you are still looking straight in front of you. Here, I'll show you. Look straight ahead," she said, holding up her hand beside me.

"Now tell me when you can see my hand," she said, as she moved her hand from behind me, to the side of my face.

"Okay, I see it now," I said excitedly, as though I had passed some big test.

I was only seven remember, anything new was a big deal to me.

"Okay, so you now know what peripheral vision is. That plays a big part, in what I am about to tell you. Some people have good peripheral vision, and some do not. It's not for us to know why we are all created differently, that's the good Lord's business. I can tell you that we have good peripheral vision, you and me. Do you ever notice something out of the corner of your eye, but when you turn your head, there is nothing there?"

"Yeah, that happens all the time," I said, excitedly.

"I figured you did. Now listen to me, most people that it happens to just dismiss it as their imagination, and honestly for most people, it probably is. Some people however, say that they see spirits that way. I can't answer if they do, or if they don't, all I know is that the people in our family with our special type of peripheral vision don't see ghosts, we see something completely different. Do you follow me so far?" she asked, before continuing.

"Yes, I suppose so."

"Good, that's good," she said, pausing to think for a few seconds.

"What I'm about to tell you is a lot for someone your age to understand, but I'm getting old and I don't know how long I have left, besides you're pretty smart for your age. When I see things out of the corner of my eye, I'm not imagining them, they are real things. They are places in the fabric of our world that are thin in those spots. That is to say, that I can see through these thin places in the fabric, from our world to another. I have this ability, as do you, and like I said before, my Dad and brother did as well."

So, that was my introduction to peripheral vision and to the existence of another world, besides our own. I was seven, so I was amazed, but I was more accepting of it than I would have been if I had been older, I think.

Grandma continued with her story about when she was young. She and her brother hid in the tall grass on top of the little knoll, overlooking the river. Her Dad was still standing on the bank of the river, looking across it to the other side. He turned his head to the left and then to the right, as if looking for something. Her brother and she kept quiet in the long grass, taking turns peeking over the hill to where their Dad stood. After a few minutes, they got bored and they lie back in the grass and started whispering, and then elbowing each other, just fooling around. When Grandma finally decided to take another peek, her Dad was gone. They stood up to get a better look but couldn't see him. From their vantage point on top of the hill, they could see for hundreds of yards in all directions. Their Dad was nowhere to be seen; it was as if he had vanished into thin air. They went down to the river's edge, to the spot where he had been standing. His footprints were still there in the soft muck by the water's edge.

The water running over the rapids was quite loud, now that they were closer to the river. The sweet smell of the tall grass was replaced by the pungent smell of the mud along its banks, mixed with the scent of algae that covered the rocks.

They thought that maybe he had crossed the river, so they went up the river to where a large tree had long since fallen from one bank to the other. They gingerly made their way across to the other side to check. There were no footprints on the other side. There was no sign of their Dad.

They got scared, thinking that maybe he had fallen in and drowned and gotten swept away with the current. They crossed back across the river and ran up the hill to go back to the house. Grandma's brother stopped to survey the land one last time, before they continued. He yelled to her to stop and come back. When she came back to the crest of the hill, she could see her Dad walking by the river's edge, a long way from where they had last seen him. They called to him and waved to him, but he didn't hear or see them. They ran down the hill to greet him, but as they approached him, he acted strangely and ran away.

"He didn't look the same, I couldn't put my finger on it, but he seemed different," Grandma said.

"Anyway, my brother and I stood there and watched as he ran away. We were confused of course, as to why he would have reacted as he did. More on that later, I have something to show you and I want to do it before your Dad comes back. It's like a special kind of magic trick, but you mustn't tell anyone about it. You have to promise that you won't tell anyone. Can you do that, Jack?"

"I promise," I said. I was excited to see her magic trick.

She looked to her left and then to her right, her head turning slowly from side to side. Her chin rose and fell as she did. She got up from the bench and walked to the edge of the water, and continued moving her head rhythmically, slowly back and forth. She stopped suddenly with her head turned to her right and her chin pointed up at the sky. What she did next, haunted me in my dreams at night, for many years after. She reached out and grabbed hold of the air in front of her, as if it was a picture on a canvas. She ripped it open and stepped through. The sound was a terrible ripping sound, like corrugated cardboard being torn and broken glass falling on a hard surface below.

She was gone, and the world closed back in, and was the same as before. I ran to the water's edge and waved my arms around, looking for an opening, but found none. I called out to her, over and over, but to no avail. Tears were streaming down my face; I was scared and confused.

Then that awful ripping, tearing sound and the sound of breaking glass, broke the still air. I looked up, and there was Grandma struggling to crawl through the tiny opening that she had ripped between the worlds.

I'm still not sure what bothered me more that day or what haunts me more. It could be the sound that it made, or the image of her going and coming back from thin air, but I think the thing that bothered me most was the look of her face.

She had been having a good day, but what crawled back through the opening was not the sweet, caring Grandma that had left minutes before. Her face was twisted and grotesque, devoid of any emotion. Her brown eyes stared vacantly through me. I asked her if she was okay, but she didn't respond. She sat on the bench and continued to stare off into the sky above my head. Tiny strands of spittle formed at the corners of her mouth, gathered and then spilled down her chin and pooled on her chest.

Then a wide grin began to spread across her face. It wasn't a happy grin; it was pure evil. Her lips pulled back like a dog baring its teeth. I had to look away; I couldn't stand the sight of it.

I looked up the lawn toward the main building and was relieved to see my Dad coming down the slope to where we were.

"How long has she been like this? I've never seen her like this," Dad asked.

"Just a couple of minutes, she was fine until a couple of minutes ago," I managed.

"I'm sorry Jack, she was having a good day. I thought that she'd be okay until I returned."

"It's okay Dad, it's not your fault."

I had just promised my Grandma that I wouldn't tell her secret, and I didn't. I kept looking over at her sitting on the bench and hoping that she would snap out of it. It scared me to see her that way.

For many years to come I had bad dreams of the events that took place on that day. I could see her twisted face and her vacant eyes staring at me. It was always the same, repeating herself again and again. Warning me not to tell anyone, our little secret.

"You promised, you promised Jacky," she would say.

In my dreams, she was always crawling into our world, and her face was always the first thing I would see. It gives me goose bumps even now, thinking about it.

Many times, over the years I came close to telling my Dad about the events of that day and about my own experiences, but I never did. I'm not sure why not. It may have been because of the promise I made to my Grandma, but that was when I was little. If he didn't believe me, I could have shown him, so yeah, not really sure. I guess that's a topic I can discuss with my therapist during my next session, if it comes up.

Anyway, we helped her to her room, tucked her in bed and went to talk to the nurse to tell her that she was no longer having a good day. I noticed that some of the pictures had been turned around to face the wall. There was a picture of her Dad, and one of her brothers that faced the room. Her Dad bore a striking resemblance to my mine. He was taller and stronger looking, but his facial features were the same. He had the same high cheekbones and thin face, with close-set eyes and a large nose. I couldn't discern the colour of his eyes because the picture was in black and white. My Dad's eyes were brown, and his hair was black then. Now his hair is mixed with grey and he has a hole in his haircut. Her Dad was healthier looking than mine, from all the hard work on the farm, and a better diet. Dad was rushed a lot of the time and ate more junk food than he should have. This explained his potbelly and it also contributed to my own weight problems as a kid. The pictures of Mom, Dad, my sister and me were all turned to face the wall. He noticed it too and stopped on the way out, to turn them around.

"I wonder why she would do that," he muttered under his breath, shaking his head.

"What do you say we go for ice cream on the way home?" Dad asked.

I think he felt guilty for leaving me alone with Grandma and was trying to atone for it. Whatever the reason, I was happy to agree to going for ice cream.

"Sounds good," I said.

We went to the Tasty Freeze. Dad and I both had the same thing, a chocolate and vanilla swirl ice cream cone. His was a large and I got a small. The creamy, cold, delicious ice cream was a welcome distraction and succeeded in helping me to forget about the events at the retirement home, at least for a while.

CHAPTER TWO

The next time I saw Grandma was at Thanksgiving. Dad went to the retirement home to pick her up and this time I stayed home. Luckily enough, she was having another good day, and there were no disappearing acts this time. I hadn't seen her since that fateful day at the retirement home and I was a bit apprehensive about seeing her now.

When they arrived, Mom and Helen went out to the car to greet them. Mom urged me to come with them, but I lagged behind. I hid behind my Mom's skirt, peeking out as the cool autumn breeze blew her skirt to one side. Helen was also wearing a skirt and it also provided me with a place to hide behind, when the wind was right. She never wore a skirt. I think it might have been the first time that I ever saw her wear one. I never noticed before, how much my Mom and sister looked alike, until that very moment. Mom had brown hair and eyes and Helen had blonde hair and blue eyes. That may be why I didn't see the resemblance. They are both tall for women, about the same height as Dad and I are presently. Of course, back then they weren't the same height, we were just kids. They both have thin faces and scant eyebrows. I was the unlucky one of the family. I was the one with a round face to go with my round physique and a dark bushy uni-brow. Lots of visits to the gym and some laser treatment have done wonders to change my outward appearance.

Anyway, back to Grandma. Dad was there to help her out of the car, but she accepted no help. She was able to navigate her way out of the car and up the steps, rather easily. Dad got her things out of the trunk, because apparently, she was staying over night. She brushed by all of us and went straight for the house.

"No time for formalities now, I'll catch up with you all later. This old bladder is going to explode if I don't hurry."

After she emerged from the bathroom, visibly refreshed, she greeted everyone with hugs and kisses. I was a little standoffish at first, but she was having a really good day, and my apprehension was melted away by her infectious smile.

We went into the living room and continued with our visit. As I said,

Grandma was a great storyteller and she had a captive audience. The time flew by, and before we knew it, dinner was nearly ready.

There was no need to prompt us. Helen and I knew what our duties were. We set the table and helped Mom with what we could. Some things were still too heavy or too hot for Helen to handle safely, so I had to do a bit more than she did. She is younger than me be by twenty months, which is a lot when you are seven. It doesn't mean much now that we are older, but I still like to call her 'youngin' just to rub it in.

We sat down to a wonderful meal with all the trimmings. There was the usual Thanksgiving Day fare such as turkey, sweet potatoes, stuffing, corn and white potatoes with gravy. My favourite was still to come. Mom made her delicious homemade apple pie that was a recipe given to her by Grandma.

"You've outdone yourself once again Irene," Grandma said, when she had finished eating.

"Well thank you for saying so Betty, I'm glad you liked it," Mom said, smiling.

"I enjoyed it very much, thank you. I don't remember the apple pie tasting that good when I made it," Grandma said.

"That's kind of you to say, thank you."

Now that supper was over, Helen and I had to help with dishes. Mom stayed with us to help clean off the table and wash the dishes and the two of us dried them. Dad and Grandma went back out to the living room to talk.

I lost interest in drying the dishes very quickly and drifted toward the living room to listen to Grandma and Dad. After a couple of minutes, Helen or Mom noticed that I was missing and one of them would come and drag me back to the kitchen. I dried a couple of dishes and then gravitated toward the living room. Mom came and dragged me back to the kitchen again. It's not that I was trying to get out of doing the dishes, but I just couldn't help myself. I was just so interested in what Grandma and Dad were talking about. I ended up having to finish the rest of the dishes by myself, while Helen was excused to go and visit with her. I hurried as fast as I could to finish the dishes and then went into the living room. They were talking about an election and who they were going to vote for. I didn't follow what they were saying, and I didn't really care. I thought that I was missing something exciting, but I was sure wrong.

After visiting for a couple of hours, Grandma said she was going to go sit out on the porch and get some fresh air.

"You care to join me Jack? I have to finish telling you the story we started, the last time you came to visit," Grandma said.

"Can I come too?" Helen asked.

"I'm sorry dear, I have to finish telling your brother the story I started. When I've finished, I'll tell you a story. Okay?"

"Okay Grandma, that sounds fair," Helen said.

"Alright Jack let's go out to the porch and I'll finish telling you my story."

So, I followed her out on to the front porch. I was a little nervous, because of what had had happened the last time I saw her. She could see that I was scared, and she did her best to set my mind at ease.

"I'm sorry Jacky, for what happened the last time. I promise, no disappearing tricks this time," she said, patting me on the top of the head.

"Now, sit here, right up close to me, so I don't have to talk too loudly," she said tapping the seat beside her.

I climbed up, sat close to her and settled in, for as it turned out, a lengthy story.

"Let me start by saying again, I'm sorry for what happened the last time we were together. I should have known better. You should know that your old Granny still has her wits about her. Although sometimes I could use better judgement, I think. I don't have Alzheimer's or dementia, or whatever they want to call it. I know what you're thinking, that you've seen it with your own eyes. Your parents and the doctors teamed up to put me in that retirement home because of it. I can't blame them, I understand. I would have done the same thing if I were in their shoes. I've caught glimpses of the other me, and it's not pretty, I get that. I guess it's my fault really, I should have been more careful," she said, pausing for a moment to collect her thoughts.

I was speechless, just sat there blinking. I was still having trouble processing all of this.

"Anyway, I'll start back where I left off previously. Do you remember where I was in the story? Wait. Any questions before I continue?" she asked.

"I have one question. Why do you keep jumping if you know the bad Grandma is going to come here?" I asked.

"Well Jacky, I'm not sure. I guess it just gets addictive. Have you ever done something that you know you probably shouldn't, but you just can't stop?" she asked.

"Like playing in the mud puddles on the way home from school? I know I'm going to get in trouble from my parents when I come home all covered in mud, but I just can't help myself," I said, beaming.

"That's exactly it. Now you know how I feel. So, do you remember where

I was in the story that I was telling you before?" she asked, smiling warmly.

"You and your brother were spying on your Father," I said.

"Oh Jacky. I wouldn't have put it quite that way, but I guess you're right. I guess we were spying on him," she said, laughing.

"Your Dad ran away from you," I recalled.

"Oh yes, that's right. Okay, let me think for a minute. I may not have dementia, but I am old just the same," she said, pausing to think.

After a minute or so, she resumed her story.

My brother and I took our time going back to the house. We were confused and a little scared, to be quite honest. We went over it and over it. Both of us telling what we saw from our point of view, and our stories matched. This confirmed that we weren't just imagining things. We had stalled long enough. We knew that our Mom would be wondering where we were by now. It was almost supper time, and we had been gone for hours. Dad was sitting in his favourite chair in the living room when we came inside. He looked up from his paper and flashed his normal toothy smile.

"Where have you been? Haven't seen you two all day," he asked.

My brother and I exchanged glances. I know we were both thinking the same thing. We had just seen him down by the river and he ran away from us. We were confused by his reaction then and we were confused by what he said now.

My Dad was a great man. He was very kind, warm-hearted, but he was strict and could be scary when he was mad or if someone crossed him. I was able to talk to my Dad easier than my brother could. I think that had something to do with me being the eldest, and a girl as well. In any case, I decided that I would talk to him after supper, when I could get him alone.

We ate supper in relative silence; my brother and I were still thinking about the events that had happened earlier in the day.

"You guys are awfully quiet. What did you guys do today? You weren't up to no good, were you?" Mom asked.

"We were just off exploring. We're just tired, I think," I responded.

"I see. Did you see anything interesting?" Mom asked.

My brother and I glanced at each other again, but Mom was looking at her plate and didn't notice.

"No, nothing out of the ordinary," I lied.

That was the end of the conversation. We finished our supper and helped clean up. My brother went to his room. He didn't want to be anywhere around Dad and I, when I talked to him about what had happened earlier in the day.

I followed Dad out onto the stoop. Every night he went out there to smoke his pipe after supper. Many nights I sat out there with him. He would talk to me about school, farming, or tell me a story. He was a good storyteller, my Dad. We were very close, closer than my Mom and me.

After several minutes of chit chat, he could see that there was something weighing heavily on me.

"Okay, out with it. I can see that there's something eating at you, and if you don't let it out, it will consume you," he said quietly, taking a long draw on his pipe and exhaling contentedly.

"When Bill and I were out exploring earlier, we saw you down by the river. You don't remember do you?"

Dad's demeanour changed immediately. His brown eyes seemed to darken and the wrinkles above them became deep furrows. He wasn't mad; I could tell that straight away, but he was deeply concerned.

"Let's go for a walk out to the barn and check on the animals," he said, as he got up and walked toward the barn.

I jumped to my feet and followed him. I knew we weren't going to check on the animals. He wanted to talk to me, where we wouldn't be disturbed. When we got into the barn, Dad lifted me and swung me up onto the top of some stacked bales of hay. From this vantage point, I was roughly the same height as him, which was quite tall. He paced back in forth in front of me for a few seconds, before he began to speak. He told me about peripheral vision and he explained to me, as I did to you, about how it ran in our family.

There was a lot of information that was passed to him from his Dad, and then there was stuff that he learned along the way.

I was as awestruck as you must have been, the day that you first found out about all this business. The nice tidy world that I had taken for granted, was shaken to its foundation.

There is at least one world that we know of, that borders our own. There may be more, but my Dad never saw another, nor have I. This other world is identical to our own physically. There are differences in the way that the governments work and social aspects, but everything else is pretty similar. There are some interesting things that were invented there, that weren't invented here.

"Do you follow me so far Jacky. Any questions?" she asked.

"I think so Grandma. Does that mean that there is another you and me, and Helen and Mom and Dad there, in the other world?"

"I knew you were smart enough to get this, even at your age. Yes, there is another you and me in the other world. There isn't another Helen or your

Mom or Dad, however. The only people that have twins, if you want to call them that; are the people like us that can travel between the two worlds. There is something else very important that you should know. There is always good and evil in our world as well as in the other world. It seems as though our twins in the other world, are opposite to us."

"So, that's why the other Grandma, that came that day at the retirement home, looked like she did?" I asked.

"Yes, that's right. Not everyone from the other world is bad. There are plenty of bad folks in our world and plenty of good folks there. They are just opposite; you understand?"

"I get it. You're good, so the other one is bad. So, that means there is a bad Jack over there as well," I said, shuddering.

"Yes, that's exactly it. You must be very careful of bad Jack. I have seen him many times, and he seems like a terror," Grandma said.

She continued her story. Her Dad told her about the other world, and how only certain people had twins in each of the two worlds. These were the only people that had peripheral vision. The rest of the people had no idea that any of this was going on. He started travelling between the worlds as a young man, before his Father told him about it. He learned later that it ran in his family. Everyone is different, but most people are able to start travelling between the worlds when they are adults. I know you are probably wondering why we even do it. I think at first, it's because we can. It's human nature to want to experience new things. It's interesting to see what things are different there and what are the same. It becomes addictive. I know for me, in the beginning, it was very hard to stay away. I always wanted to travel, but it interferes with having a normal life here. I tried to limit myself to travelling there once a week. Once I had a family and responsibilities, it was easier to stay away, because I was very busy.

"Now you understand why my Dad ran away from us on that day, why he didn't seem to recognize us. It was because it wasn't my Dad at all, but his twin," Grandma said.

"No, I get it. It's the same as the bad Grandma that I saw at the retirement home. Does that mean that the other man that looked like your Dad was bad?" I asked.

"Oh, that's a good question. I guess I gave that impression. There are definitely those that are complete opposites, like my twin and me. I think you will have to watch the other Jack as well; he seems to be a bad apple. There are others though, that just have different characteristics. One might be shy or timid, while the other might be bold and outspoken. One might have blond hair, the other might have black hair; that kind of thing. So, to answer your question; no. The man that looked like my Father turned out to be an okay guy."

"You have to be extra careful when you start to travel Jacky. I have a bad feeling about that other Jack. He could cause all sorts of trouble for you. Promise me, you'll be careful," she said.

"I promise Grandma," I said, but I had no idea what I was in store for.

I was so lost in thought, that I didn't hear Jason open the car door and get in. One of my charming nicknames as a kid was as I said earlier, space cadet. It wasn't inaccurate, but it was cruel nevertheless. I'm old enough now that I can understand why some kids called me that, but at the time it still hurt. I'd love to say that I'm over it, but that would be a bold - faced lie. It has affected me, as does everything, whether it is good or bad. I know that is why I chose the career path that I did, and Helen too, for that matter.

"Having a little nap with your eyes open again?" Jason teased.

"Huh? What? No, I was just thinking about my Grandma. It is her birthday today," I said.

"She died when you and Helen were teenagers, didn't she? Helen said she never really knew her, because of her dementia," he said.

"Yeah, I guess so," I responded.

"Well, I got the rest of the stuff for our camping trip, last one of the summer before school starts. I can't believe that summer's over already," Jason said, shaking his head.

"Yeah, I know what you mean. I have to go back to work in two weeks," I said.

"Vicki isn't joining us?"

"No. I guess Helen didn't tell you. Vicki and I broke up a couple of days ago," I said, glumly.

"No, she didn't say anything. That's too bad. We really liked her. We both thought that she was the one."

"Me too, but I still haven't given up hope. She may come around yet."

"I hope you're right, I thought that she was good for you. What happened between you two, if you don't mind me asking?" Jason asked.

"I don't mind you asking. I'm just not going to tell you," I said, smiling wryly.

"Fair enough, a little too soon I guess."

I didn't respond. That conversation was over, as far as I was concerned. We sat in silence for the rest of the ride to Jason and Helen's house. It wasn't awkward. It actually felt nice, to not have to fill the silence with meaningless chatter. He and I have known each other for years. I wouldn't say we were friends before he and Helen met, but we were acquaintances. Now, we have a very good relationship.

When we arrived at their house, she was just getting home from work and the boys were playing out back. I said hello to my sis and then went into the backyard to see my nephews. Brian and Nate were throwing a football back and forth. Nate threw it in my direction, when he saw me come through the gate to the back yard. I caught it and threw my arms into the air, as if to signal a touchdown.

"You should have played football Uncle Jack. I bet you would have made an awesome tight end," Brian said, as he ran over to meet me, followed by Nate.

"No, I don't think so. Haven't you ever seen pictures of me when I was younger?" I said laughing and giving them both hugs.

I could see how they might think that I would have made a good football player. I am six foot and about 205 pounds, now. In high school, I was about as round as I was tall. I had a bad acne problem from all the junk food I ate, and sports weren't high on my list of things to do. So, that's where I got the other charming nicknames, fatty and pimples. Like I said before, kids can be cruel. Nate and Brian never saw me like that. Nate and Brian are 10 and 8 respectively, and never saw the out of shape me. I was shorter than most kids my age, until I experienced a late growth spurt, just prior to my eighteenth birthday. So, that led me to play basketball, develop a little self-esteem and allowed me to make some friends.

"I've seen pictures of you when you were little, but none after that," Brian said.

I wasn't surprised. Pictures were taken less and less frequently as I got heavier, and the acne got worse. My parents knew that I hated having my picture taken, so they refrained from it. At some point, I destroyed any pictures, that they did take during that time.

"Well let's just say, I haven't always been as fit as I am now," I said.

We settled into throwing the football around and catching up a bit. I hadn't seen the boys for a couple of days because of the problems that I had been having with Vicki. Jason came and joined us in the backyard, after he had finished putting the groceries away. My troubles were forgotten, and I just enjoyed spending time with him and the kids.

"We thought that we could have supper and then get to bed early, get an early start first thing tomorrow. You're welcome to stay here if you want," Jason said.

"Yeah, you know, that sounds like a good idea. A change of scenery will do me good, thanks."

"No problema, mi casa es su casa," he said, in his best Spanish accent.

"I figured we could load up all the camping gear and the canoe tonight, then we just have to grab the coolers in the morning. We can eat an early breakfast and then hit the road," Jason said.

"Sounds good to me. I'm going to go see if Helen needs any help with supper," I said, as I threw the ball to Brian and then walked toward the back door.

"What's up sis?" I asked, when I got into the kitchen.

She had her head buried in the refrigerator and jumped a little, bumping her head in the process.

"Shit, you scared me. I didn't hear you come in," she said.

"Sorry," I said, laughing a little.

"Can I help with anything?"

"Sure, you can find the romaine lettuce. There's too much shit in here and I can't find it, and my fucking back hurts. And yes, before you say anything, I AM having a bad day," she said loudly.

"Okay, not a problem. Let me have a look see," I said, ignoring her cursing.

I knew my sister very well and I knew that her bad moods didn't last long, if you stayed out of her way and let her work through it on her own.

I found the romaine lettuce hiding behind the bag of milk. I grabbed a bowl, cut up the lettuce and mushrooms, added some bacon bits and croutons, then got the dressing from the refrigerator. I mixed it all together and then got a bottle of wine and poured Helen a glass and handed it to her. She took a sip, let out a sigh and sunk into a chair by the table.

"Thanks, big brother, I needed that."

"I've known you long enough to know, stay out of your way when you're in a bad mood," I said, chuckling.

We ate supper, and as planned, we got to bed early. It was a long drive to the campground we were going to, so we had to get an early start. I went to bed when they did, but I couldn't sleep. I lie in bed, looking at the ceiling. I didn't want to wake the others, so I stayed that way, until I was confident everyone was fast asleep. I climbed out of bed and crept quietly through the house and out the front door. I walked around the block twice, and I still wasn't tired. I sat down on a bus stop bench and thumbed through my contacts until I found Vicki's number. It was only ten o'clock, so I knew she would still be awake. I dialed her number and listened to the phone ringing in my ear. It rang once, twice, three times, four times, five times. I was about to hang up, then she answered, half way through the sixth ring.

"Hi jack," Vicki said. I could tell by the sound of her voice, that she was tired.

"Hi Vick. I'm sorry for calling. I just wanted to hear your voice."

"I'm glad you called. I've been doing some thinking. I love you, there's no denying that. I won't pretend that I don't, and I know that you love me too. I'm just not sure if that's enough. Go camping with your family and when you get back, let's spend some time apart. I mean don't stop by or call or anything. I mean really apart. When you figure out what is going on with you, then call me and we can talk." Vicki said, then exhaled loudly.

"Okay Vick, I love you," I said, to a dial tone ringing in my ear. She had hung up already, but that was okay I guess. It was nice to hear her voice just the same.

CHAPTER THREE

The next morning came faster than any of us would have liked, especially for me. The last time I looked at the clock it was 12:15 a.m., and it was now 5:30 a.m. When I crawled back in bed, I stared at the ceiling for another hour or so, thinking about the events of the last couple of months. I should have known better, Grandma warned me. To my defence though, I was younger at the time and suffered as most of us do, from a sense of invincibility. To be honest, I had forgotten about it until things had started to go a wry. I had promised her that I would be careful. I can't say that I have been. I've been careless, if anything. I'm not so sure if I could have changed things; short of travelling that is. Travelling is definitely like a drug. It's hard to stop once you start, and it seems to hurt the people around you, as much or more than it hurts you.

In any case, I have a few minutes to spare, waiting for the other four to finish breakfast. I know I should eat something, but I have no appetite this morning. It's too early. My thoughts drift to Grandma again. She never did tell anyone but me, about her travelling. I'm not sure why, but it was our little secret and I haven't told another soul either. I guess I didn't want to worry anyone, or maybe I wanted it to be something special between my Grandma and me. I hadn't given it much thought, until recently. I do know, that it I have to tell someone, and that someone is going to be Helen, this week. It should have been Vicky... long ago.

She went on to tell me about some of the things that she had learned from years of travelling. Her twin was an evil person and she was constantly getting into scrapes with the law. Once, Grandma almost ended up in jail because of her and had it not been for a fortunate set of circumstances, she could have. When she was younger, her twin was arrested for stealing a car, possession of drugs and several assaults. Luckily for her, Geandma wasn't around to take the fall.

"You have to understand Jacky. Nobody would know the difference between you and your twin. If they do something bad, you could get blamed for it. So, you have to be extra careful. I know I've said that many times, but it's very important," Grandma said, with earnest.

"Okay, I understand," I said.

I did think that I understood, but how could I fully comprehend what I was up against? It was a case of not knowing how much I didn't know.

It's funny, how I can remember so much about that conversation with Grandma, so many years ago. I was seven at the time, and to me she was ancient. She was in fact only 61. She officially died at 70 from Alzheimer's, but I continued to visit her for many years after that. She must have had her reasons for not telling anyone she was still alive. I never asked her, and she never offered an explanation. I remember wanting so badly to tell everyone at the funeral, but she made me promise not to. It's not very likely that anyone would have believed me anyway.

Grandma was waiting for me after school one day. She walked with me for a bit. We talked, and she told me where to find her, when I started to travel. I was sixteen and I didn't see her again for another three years.

I remember, like it was yesterday. The lowly lit room of the funeral parlour, the strong fragrance of flowers that filled the small space. The smell was so strong, that it made it hard for me to breathe. I took little shallow breaths, trying to avoid the smell. Eventually I became accustomed to it and it ceased to bother me. The room was separated into two sections. There was a small section at the front where the casket sat, surrounded by flowers and cards and pictures of her, from all stages of her life. There were large French doors that were open to the larger room at the back. In the larger one were chairs and sofas lining the edges. They were all beige and covered with a busy floral pattern. Their legs were intricately carved, dark stained wood. At the back of the room, hanging in the centre of the wall, was a picture of Queen Elizabeth II.

It was the first funeral I had ever been to. There were streams of people coming past the casket at the front of the room, offering their condolences to Dad and Mom. Helen and I spent the majority of the time, sitting at the back, on one of the sofas. Helen shed some tears, but she really didn't know Grandma all that well. It was usually Dad and I that went to visit her at the retirement home. Mom usually stayed behind to take her to gymnastics or dance or something. In fact, there weren't a lot of tears shed at her funeral. Don't get me wrong, she was a well - liked person, but she had been in the retirement home for several years and had lost touch with many of the people that knew her. Most people were sad of course, but they counted it as a blessing that she could now be at peace and not struggle with Alzheimer's any longer. The process on the other hand fascinated me, but I was certainly not sad. Oh, I guess I was sad, that I wouldn't be able to see her until I started travelling.

It was a surreal experience, seeing Grandma's twin in the casket. I did feel a twinge of sadness, but it was quickly replaced with disdain for the woman that was lying there. This woman had caused my Grandma so much grief over her lifetime that it was hard to feel sorry for her. I guess I also felt sad, thinking that when she did die for real, I would be the only one from our family there.

"Are you awake, or are you sleeping with your eyes open again?" Helen said, from the doorway.

"Hmm, yeah I'm awake. I was just thinking about Grandma."

"I see. Anything in particular?"

"I was just thinking about her funeral."

"What made you think of that?" she asked.

"It was her birthday yesterday, and I've been thinking about her a lot lately."

"You were always closer to her than anyone else, weren't you?" Helen asked, sounding puzzled.

"I suppose so."

"And why do you suppose that was?" she asked.

"Well, that's part of what I want to talk to you about?" I said.

"About what? I know something is going on with you."

"Not now. We'll talk this weekend, when we can be alone for a couple of hours."

"Okay, but I'm holding you to it. Something is definitely up with you. Anyway, we're ready to hit the road."

"I'm ready," I said, springing from the bed and walking toward the door.

I helped Jason carry the coolers out to the truck. There wasn't enough room in the back, so we had to re-arrange things so that they would fit. Once that was done, we were ready to hit the road. I sat in the back with the kids. Brian and Nate sat together on one side and I sat on the other. They were busy playing on their tablet and I looked out the window. That was okay with me; I didn't feel much like talking anyway. I couldn't stop thinking about my Grandma. I was the only one that knew how close we were. No one else in the family would have guessed how strong our bond had become. They didn't know about her travelling and about her living past her seventieth birthday, as I did. I felt a certain bond that they couldn't, and I felt a little sad that they didn't fully know her, as I did.

It was a long drive, but I won't bore you with the details. The real point of this trip was to talk to Helen about all of this. It would be a hard sell, but once I gave her a demonstration, she'd have to believe. How she would take the news, that her Brian had the 'gift'; well, that was another story.

The campsite and the surrounding area couldn't have been better. Our campsite was on a small hill overlooking the entire lake. It wasn't a large lake, maybe four hundred acres or so, but it had little fingers that jutted out in several directions. It was perfect for exploring and it had the look of a real northern lake, even though we were only a few hours drive from the city. The water was tea stained in colour and it was a bit on the cool side. A small river ran into the end of the lake, not far from where our campsite was. I could hear the water bubbling over the rocks at the bottom of the small dam. There was a man and a boy, about Nate's age, fishing where the fast water met the calm of the lake. They waved when they saw me looking in their direction.

The lake itself was like a mirror. There wasn't a ripple on its surface and the trees that surrounded it were reflected back at me, making the colour of the water appear to be green. A loon out in the middle of the lake cried out its lonely song. It brought to mind, all the things that I truly loved about camping. The sound of a loon on a lake, was number one on my list of favourite things, closely followed by the smell of the various campfires. Watching a fire at night was also high on my list, along with swimming and fishing of course. The peace and tranquility were very welcome things, especially with the start of the new school year, looming in the not so distant future.

I sat at the picnic table for a moment, closed my eyes and inhaled deeply. The smell of campfires and evergreen filled my nose. I took another deep breath and savoured the wonderful smells and wondered why it was, that I didn't make a point of coming camping more often. I had reached a point in my life, that I wanted to make some changes. I was going to make a list of things that I needed to start doing, and changes that I wanted to make in my life. Why not start with, camping more often?

I had been sitting idle long enough. I thought I had better help Jason and Helen unpack the truck. Nate and Brian were nowhere to be seen; down by the water exploring, no doubt. Jason was untying the canoe and I finished helping him. We left it in the back of the truck and grabbed the coolers and set them on the picnic table.

Nate and Brian weren't the only ones interested in going to explore the lake and check out our surroundings.

"What do ya say we go check out the lake, this stuff will still be here when we get back?" Jason called to Helen.

"I suppose you could twist my arm," she said, as she ran toward the lake.

I followed behind but took a different path. It was a perfect vantage point to see the entire lake, absolutely breathtaking. Helen and Jason were just a few yards up the shoreline. He had caught up to her and now they were standing overlooking the lake, holding each other lovingly. I was happy to see that they were still very much in love, but I wished that I could share this with Vicki. I could only hope, that one day I would be able to do so.

Nate and Brian were a little farther up the shoreline and they waved enthusiastically for me to come see what they had found. I made my way down to where they were, being careful not to slip on the algae covered rocks. Nate was holding a huge bullfrog and Brian was grinning. The bullfrog didn't seem to be quite as happy as the two of them, so I persuaded them to let him go. Nate went up on to the grass and set him down.

"Can you get a picture with Brian and me?" he asked, as he pulled Brian beside him.

I pulled out my phone, lay down on the grass and held the phone out in front of me. From this vantage point the bullfrog was enormous in the foreground. The boys had huge smiles on their faces when I snapped the picture. The bullfrog cooperated perfectly and didn't jump away, until after the picture was taken. The boys never saw the frog leave. They were too intent on seeing the picture that I had taken. They laughed, high - fived each other and then me, when they saw the picture. I must admit; it did turn out to be a great picture.

Helen and Jason were making their way back to the campsite, so I gathered up the boys and carried them back. They were squirming and making a fuss, but I could tell that they were enjoying the ride. I set them down by the picnic table and went to the back of the truck to retrieve some supplies.

"You two can start putting up your tent," Jason said to the boys.

"Okay Dad," they said, and got right to work.

They had been camping several times a year, for as long as they could remember and by now they were seasoned veterans. They had their tent up in less time than it took me to put up mine.

"Geez, what's taking you so long Uncle Jack?" Brian teased.

"Yeah, yeah, I'm getting it, don't hassle me," I said, laughing.

We set up camp and relaxed for a few minutes. Jason and Helen emerged from their tent with their bathing suits on. Brian and Nate took one look and disappeared into their tent, emerging a minute later with their swim shorts on.

"You coming swimming Uncle Jack?" the boys asked, in perfect unison.

"I'll meet you there."

I couldn't ask for better company or better scenery. I just couldn't shake my melancholy mood. The situation between Vicki and I was weighing heavily on my mind and I just wasn't able to get past it. There was nothing I could do about it right now. I knew that but knowing didn't make it any easier. I needed to find a way to just enjoy the moment and not worry so much about things that I couldn't change. That was easier said then done. I found myself wishing that I could go visit my Grandma. She always had good advice for me and I missed her. I never really knew how much, until the last few weeks. She was always a pillar of support for me, and now she was gone.

I shook my head a bit hoping it would help. It didn't, but I got up anyway, changed into my swim shorts and met the other four down at the lake. The cool water helped clear my mind and the infectious sound of the kids laughing, lightened my mood. Before too long, my troubles were forgotten, and I was truly enjoying myself for the first time in weeks. I splashed and laughed with the kids and had a great time. There was a large rock face about ten feet above the water's surface that we took turns jumping from. We started with cannon balls and progressed to diving and finally to somersaults, as we became braver. Jason and Helen sat close by watching, and occasionally yelling words of encouragement.

When we were sufficiently tired and waterlogged, we went back to camp, dried off and got ready to start supper.

Jason made a fire with wood that the boys had collected, and were still collecting in the woods, all around the campsite. Helen sat beside me and we chatted for a while, about nothing of any great significance. I was waiting for tomorrow, when I could be alone with her, to talk to her about the important stuff. For now, I was content to just spend the day with the four of them and especially to enjoy some alone time with my sister. Supper consisted of hamburgers and hotdogs and some potato salad that we had picked up at the grocery store. It was simple but delicious nonetheless. Food cooked over an open flame always tastes better than cooked any other way.

After supper, we went up to the main meeting area where they had a campfire sing-along for the kids. There was the five of us and two other families that had two kids each. There were two college girls that were working there for the summer, and they oversaw the campfire, story telling and sing-along.

We arrived just as the sun was slipping behind the trees. We all sat up close to the fire on logs that served as chairs. The girls were just finishing with their preparations and making sure that the fire was burning well. When they were positive that the fire had taken hold, they sat down with us and introduced themselves. They gave each of us an opportunity to introduce ourselves and then they started their presentation. They gave us some fun facts and history of the park and about the flora and fauna that could be found here. They began with a ghost story that had the children scared and holding on to their parents for dear life. By now, it was pitch black and the darkness added to the spookiness of the story. After the story was finished, they ended with a couple of campfire songs to lighten the mood. All the kids had a chance to participate and add their own twist to the song that they sang. The adults were also encouraged to join in, which I did hesitantly. The song got sillier as it went along, until it finally broke down, into a fit of laughter. A great time was had by all. We finished the night by roasting marshmallows and then watching the fire for a while, before heading back to the campsite.

The girls put the fire out and now it was completely dark. The sky was clear, and the stars shone brighter than back in town. We all stopped for a couple of minutes to look up and marvel at just how many stars were above us. It was truly a humbling experience, to see the vastness and beauty of the heavens laid out before us. We continued along the path to our campsite. Our eyes were now fully adjusted to the dark and so we could see reasonably well. Everything was still dark and cast in shadows, but it was still possible to see probably fifteen feet in front of us.

When we arrived at the campsite, there were by my count, twelve raccoons running around and trying to get into our food. The boys were delighted to see so many raccoons, but Helen, Jason and I were more concerned about keeping our food safe. Jason and I put the two coolers on the ground and then placed the bench part of the picnic table on top so that they couldn't get at our food in the middle of the night.

It had been a long day and we were all ready for bed. I said good night and crawled into my tent and was asleep almost immediately. It was the first time that had happened in months. I awoke with a start. The tell - tale sound of the zipper on my tent being opened broke the stillness of the night. I sat there dumb - founded, looking at the front of my tent. Who could be opening the door to my tent? I was half asleep, and it never occurred to me to say anything. After a few seconds, I saw a wet little nose glistening in the moonlight. Two small hands appeared through the door and began rummaging around in my duffle bag by the door. I kicked at the covers and the raccoon went scurrying away. I laughed a little to myself. My heart was actually beating faster than normal. I closed the zipper and lie back down. Stars overhead shone through the mesh in the top of the tent and the brightness of the moon illuminated the inside so much, that I could see perfectly. Great, I thought, I'll never get back to sleep now! The fresh air and the tranquility of this place must have worked its magic. I fell right back to sleep and didn't wake up until I heard the clang of a frying pan on the fire outside my tent.

"Good morning," I said, to whoever was outside my tent.

"Good morning sleepy head," Helen returned, cheerfully.

I crawled to the door of my tent and unzipped the front. The sound of the zipper reminded me of my visitor from last night and I chuckled to myself. I peaked my head through the opening, out into the cool, fresh morning air. I inhaled deeply. The air smelled fresh and pure. The wind swirled ever so slightly, bringing with it the smell of the fire, on which Helen had begun to fry some bacon. I inhaled deeply again, enjoying the smell of the fire and the bacon.

"Did you sleep well?" Helen asked.

"Like a rock," I said cheerfully.

"Me too, must be the fresh air."

"Yeah, I haven't slept like that in months. Jason and the kids out fishing?"

"No, they just went down by the water to fart around a bit before breakfast."

"Oh, I see. Can I give you a hand with anything?"

"No thanks, got it covered."

I went over to the picnic table and lifted the edge of it to remove the remaining cooler from underneath. I sat down and rubbed at my eyes. I was having difficulty waking up, fully.

"You still tired?" Helen asked.

"No. I'm just having a hard time waking up. I haven't been sleeping well for a while. I guess I'm just not used to sleeping so soundly. I was out like a light last night."

"I see. So, did you want to talk about it?" she asked.

I knew what she meant. I knew she wasn't referring to my sleeping habits. She was referring to what had been troubling me lately.

"I do want to talk about it, very much in fact. That's a big reason why I came along on this camping trip. Well, other than wanting to spend time with my little sis's family of course," I said, laughing.

"Okay, so out with it."

"Oh no, not right now. I figure we could talk while Jason and the kids are off fishing. I don't want to be interrupted, and it's going to take some time."

"Okay, I guess. It sounds serious," she said, a worried look creeping across her face.

"I just don't want to be disturbed, that's all."

"Good morning," Jason called, as he walked up the hill from the water.

"Good morning."

"Good morning Uncle Jack," the boys yelled, as they ran past.

I was lost in thought now. I was trying to figure out, what I was going to say to my sister. I guess I would just have to start at the beginning.

CHAPTER FOUR

We finished breakfast and Jason and the kids took off to go fishing. I was alone at last with Helen. This was what I had been waiting for, but now that the time had come, I was dreading having this conversation. I helped her clean up the mess from breakfast. I took as long as I could. I was in no hurry to begin the conversation about Grandma and travelling and bad Jack.

"So, are you done stalling?" Helen said in a low voice, almost whispering.

"Is it that obvious? I guess I am stalling. It's just that I don't know where to start," I said, sighing heavily.

"Just start. You can think about what you want to say as you go along, but just start," she said in a soothing, nurturing voice.

"You asked for it. I'll start at the beginning I guess. That's a long way back, but it makes the most sense to start there."

She sat in one of the fold - up chairs across from me. I got up and grabbed one of the others and pulled it up closer, so that I was facing her.

"I don't want anyone else to hear what I'm about to tell you. They'd probably take me away in a straight jacket if they heard," I said, taking a deep breath.

"I'm sure it isn't that bad. Whatever it is, I'm here for you. We'll figure it out; we always have," she said, reaching over and squeezing my hand.

"I'm going to start at the beginning. You will have a lot of questions and you probably won't believe me at first. You may want to have me committed but try to keep an open mind. Anyway, here goes. It all started when we went to see Grandma at the retirement home one spring day when I was seven. Dad had to leave me alone with her for a while so that he could do some paper work. She was completely lucid that day. Actually, as it turned out, she never had Alzheimer's at all."

"Okay, I have to interrupt. What do you mean; she didn't have Alzheimer's? I saw it for myself. That's a big part of the reason that I never really got to know her."

"There are two ways I could go here; for the shock factor, or you can pretend I didn't say that for now and I can continue with the story. Which do you prefer?" I asked.

"Never mind. I take that back. I'm continuing with the story. You'll see soon enough where I'm going with it. Grandma started to tell me a story that day about her Dad. She said that her Dad, her brother and her all had a special type of peripheral vision. As it turned out, they could all see into parallel worlds. I have that ability as well, and I suspect that Nate does too," I said, and then Helen cut me off again.

"Stop right there! First you tell me that she didn't have Alzheimer's and now you start talking about parallel worlds. Then if that's not bad enough, you try to drag Nate into this. I'm not sure what's happening with you, but I am sure, I don't like it," she said, breathing heavily, her face flushing red.

"Okay, I'm sorry. I'll have to show you the same way that Grandma showed me. You won't believe me otherwise."

I got up from my chair and surveyed the air around me in a slow circle, spinning to my left. It wasn't always easy to find a spot to enter the other world. In fact, sometimes there just weren't any at all. I did manage to find one after several minutes of looking. I didn't want to do what Grandma did and disappear completely. I figured I would just rip an opening and let Helen look through.

"Come stand beside me. I'll create an opening and I want you to look through. Don't go in, just look. Okay?" I said sternly.

"I don't know what you are talking about Jack. Stop it! You are scaring me. There are no parallel worlds. Neither Grandma, nor you, nor Nate can travel between them. Whatever it is, it'll be alright. We can get you help," she said, crying.

I reached up to find the opening without acknowledging what she had said. Actions would definitely prove more valuable than words, in this situation. I grabbed hold of the edges of the fabric and began to tear. The awful sound of ripping cardboard and broken glass filled the air. No matter how many times I heard it, I would never get used to it.

She screamed in horror and covered her ears, to shelter them from the sound. I beckoned her closer to look, which she did very hesitantly. She peeked over my shoulder and into the other world, through the space that I had created. Her hands fell from her ears and covered her mouth, but still a loud gasp escaped her. She looked from me to the hole and back again. Utter disbelief was painfully displayed across her face. I let go of the edges and the hole filled back in. There were only trees and air and the surrounding campsite again. No evidence remained of the hole that had been there, moments before.

I had first experienced this spectacle at seven, and at seven, we still believe in magic and the boogeyman and other fantastical things. To find out that there are parallel worlds seemed kind of cool and not all that strange. To find out at 28 that there are parallel worlds and that there are people that you know that can travel between them, must be mind-blowing. I could tell from Helen's reaction, that yes, it was mind-blowing.

She stood there for several minutes with her hands over her mouth. She looked from me to the spot where the hole was, moments before. She did this repeatedly, back and forth. She went to sit down in the chair that I had been sitting in, so that she was able to look at the spot where the hole had been. Her head shook back and forth, and her eyes were wide in disbelief. I let her be for a couple of minutes; letting her process this new information, before trying to talk to her.

"Are you all right Helen?" I asked. I could tell that she was decidedly not all right, but I had to start somewhere.

"Hmm," she managed.

Her eyes were still wide, and she was staring at the spot where the hole had been. She was blinking, so that was a good sign, I guess.

I walked up to her and grabbed both her hands in mine and squeezed them smartly. That seemed to do the trick. It snapped her out of the spell that she had been under.

"Ouch! That hurt. What the hell!" she said, scowling.

"Welcome back. I thought you might go catatonic on me," I said.

"I wouldn't have believed it, if I hadn't seen it with my own two eyes," she said, still shaking her head.

"I figured as much. That's why I had to show you," I said, smiling.

"I thought you were going crazy. I never would have believed it, if I hadn't seen it."

"You said that all ready," I said, laughing.

She had recovered from the initial shock, to see a little humour in the situation. Just a little.

"I must have looked like I had just seen a ghost. Wait a minute. You said that you thought that Nate might have this ability as well. What makes you think that?" she asked, worry creeping back into her voice.

"I'm not entirely positive, but I think I can see it in his eyes. Ask him if he sees things out of the corners of his eyes. That would tell you for sure; or you could just let it lie for now, until he gets older."

"I think it's best if we just let it be for now. Let's deal with what's going on with you first. What is going on with you? Go ahead and finish your story."

"Okay, I'll start back with Grandma because that's where it started for me. What I am about to tell you will shock you almost as much as what I have already showed you."

"I doubt that very much, but then I never expected what you just showed me either. Go ahead and continue and if I have questions or I need a break, then I'll stop you. Fair enough?"

"Sounds fair to me. Okay, now back to Grandma. First of all, she didn't have Alzheimer's, like I started to say before. Her twin from the other world had Alzheimer's. It was her that we buried thirteen years ago, not our real Grandma. She died just over a year ago."

I could see that she was reeling from this new information, but to her credit, she didn't interrupt me. I continued with the story.

"Grandma told me that not everyone in our world has a twin in the other world. Only those that can travel between the worlds are twins. She also said that the twins may look alike, but they are usually opposites. This may mean subtle things such as likes or sexuality or big differences such as good or evil. In her case, her twin was pure evil. Unfortunately, it seems that my twin is evil as well," I said, pausing to let Helen ask a question.

"Why did she let us believe that she was dead? She should have told us, the same as she told you," she asked.

"I'm not sure. I've always questioned that myself and she never offered an explanation either."

"Grandma told me on several occasions to watch out for bad Jack. That's what she called my twin. She said he was a devious little bugger as a kid and that I was going to have to be careful. She told me about the other world as much as she could. I was still a kid, and so I wasn't able to travel to the other world yet. Everyone is different, but most people can't travel until they are adults. I started to travel about four years after her twin died. She told me how to find her once I passed through to the other world. I would go visit her regularly," I said, pausing, because I could hear the clang of the canoe and paddles coming from the lake.

"I guess we'll continue this later then?" Helen asked.

"I guess so."

Jason, Nate and Brian ambled up the slope toward the campsite. Jason was carrying a couple of nice size small mouth bass and the boys were struggling to remove their life jackets.

"How was the fishing?" I asked.

"It wasn't too bad. We caught quite a few, but most of them were too small to keep. Nate and Brian caught these two," Jason said, holding up the bass for us to see.

"Those two love anything to do with the outdoors, don't they?" I said.

"Yeah, they aren't your typical kids, these days. When we were young we spent all our time outdoors. Most kids today spend all their time indoors," Jason said.

"Yeah, that's a good thing for sure. Those two definitely march to their own drum," I said.

"I'm going to go clean these fish, wash up and have a beer, I think," Jason said.

"It's only ten thirty in the morning," Helen said.

"I know, but I've been up for hours, besides I'm on holidays."

"I'm just teasing you. Get one for me and Jack too, when you come back, please. We're on holidays too, you know," she said.

"I could use a beer, after the morning I've had," she said to me.

"I'll second that," I said.

Nate and Brian were a little way off, turning over logs to look for salamanders. They saw their Dad heading down to the water, so they stopped what they were doing to run and catch up with him.

It was obvious that she wanted to continue our conversation from before. It was just about killing her, that she had to wait until we were alone again.

Jason returned from cleaning the fish and handed Helen and me a beer. We enjoyed our beers while he told us about their fishing adventure. I could tell that she was only half listening to his story. She was thinking about another one, of that I was certain. I knew that she wouldn't be able to think about anything else, until I finished my story.

She got her chance later that day. Jason and the boys went out fishing again. They were no sooner in the water and Helen pulled her chair up close to me and nearly begged for me to continue.

"Okay, continue. I won't be able to enjoy this camping trip, until I know the whole story. I can't believe what I've heard so far. It's just so incredible," she said.

"I know. Where did I leave off?"

"You were talking about how our real Grandma was still alive, up until a year ago and you would go to visit her, which I'm pissed about by the way, but continue," she said anxiously.

I told her about my many trips to go see her in the other world. It was amazingly similar to our world. If you didn't pay attention to politics or entertainment, then you might not even notice a difference. When she did die, I was there by her side. She didn't have to go through it alone, but it was a hard thing for me to have to deal with on my own. There was no one I could confide in, no one to lean on. Grandma and I had become very close. We always had that special bond that we shared, but it became stronger over the years. I continued to go to her house for some time afterward, but that world seemed so empty without her and I stopped going there for a while. Eventually, I did continue to go there and began to enjoy my visits again. Think of it as going on vacation, whenever you wanted to. It was quite peaceful. There was no way that anyone could reach me while I was there. There were times however, that I was mistaken for bad Jack. Those instances usually didn't go very well. Apparently other people disliked him about as much as Grandma and I did.

"I have a question. You said that only the people that have twins in the other world can travel between the two worlds. When you were holding the hole open for me to look, would I be able to go through?" Helen asked.

"I'm not sure. I've never heard of anyone trying it."

"And Grandma. How did she die?"

"It was just old age catching up with her. She had a pretty good run health wise, until about two months before she died. She started having problems getting around and she just went downhill quickly from there. I think she was fine with it at the end. She had lived a full life and she was okay with dying."

"So, let's get to the heart of the matter. You've been living this double life for most of your life. Again, that pisses me off, but... What's changed, that has you all out of sorts?" she asked.

"Ah, the million - dollar question. Remember when I said that people start travelling at different ages? Well I started travelling at a relatively young age. Bad Jack is a late bloomer however. He has only recently started to travel, and he has had several encounters with Vicki. Nothing too terrible, but I worry about what he is capable of. She didn't know it was him. She thought it was me and so she thinks I've gone off my rocker."

"Why didn't you just explain to her about the other world, like you did to me?" Helen asked.

"I guess it was because I've never told anyone any of this before. I was worried about what she would think. By the time that I decided to show her, the damage was done," I said, exhaling loudly.

"I don't believe that for a second. If you show her like you showed me, she'll understand. There's no doubt she will be freaked out, but I think she would come around," she said emphatically.

"I guess you're right. What do I have to lose at this point?"

"Exactly. So, when we get home, go talk to Vicki, or better yet show her. She'll understand."

"The only problem is, that the last time we spoke, she made it very clear that she wants some space."

"That's okay. Give her some space for now. Be patient and things will work out just fine."

"I guess you're right. I just hate the way things are between us now."

"So, we have a solution to that problem. What are we going to do with this bad Jack of yours?" Helen asked.

"I don't know what I can do about him. When I travel, I try to blend in and not draw attention to myself. He doesn't seem to care, and I worry about what he will do, and then I'll suffer the consequences."

"Let me think about it. Don't worry about it big brother, we'll figure it out."

I liked her positive attitude. I could use more of that right now. I had fallen into quite the funk recently. All that had been going on with me and the situation with Vicki had really been weighing on me. It was time to take back my life, but I wasn't always a take charge kind of person. I think it goes back to my childhood and the relentless teasing I endured because of my appearance.

CHAPTER FIVE

Growing up I was always a very shy kid. I'm not sure at this point which came first, the teasing or my shyness. It may have been that I was shy because of the continual teasing. I was a chubby kid when I was growing up. Back then it was considered normal for children to tease other kids. There wasn't the harassment and bullying awareness that there is today. They now realize how damaging it can be and try to educate kids, so that it doesn't happen. I could have told them how damaging it was. All they had to do was ask.

Anyway, it was a vicious circle. The more I was teased, the more I ate and the fatter I became and the more I was teased. Let's just say I had a miserable childhood.

I was ashamed of myself and so I became quiet and withdrawn. I didn't have any friends and I was sad a lot of the time. As I got older, my parents would let me go off on my own. I told them that I was going to a friend's house, and then I would ride out to see Grandma at the retirement home. I guess I wasn't lying. She was a great friend to me. That's why she and I became so close. I spent a lot more time with her growing up, then anyone knew. It was our little secret, just like the other secret that we shared.

I remember one particular incident that happened when I was ten. I was on my way to school. It was a short walk, so my parents let me go on my own. I had to walk down the street for a couple of blocks and then cut through a small wooded area. There was a large manicured trail that led to the back of the schoolyard. I was wearing my new baseball hat that my Dad had just bought me on the weekend. It was Monday morning and I was so proud to wear it to school and show it off. It was a beautiful autumn morning. The leaves were still on the trees but had begun to turn brilliant hues of reds, oranges and yellows. The strong smell of leaves was everywhere in the cool autumn air. I was wearing a light pullover jacket and I was carrying my favourite Scooby-Doo lunch box. For me, this was as good as life got.

I was earlier leaving for school that day than normal. I was so excited to show off my new hat. I was thinking about how happy it made me feel and I took it off and rolled it over in my small hands. I examined every stitch, every seam. I felt the soft material and looked at the emblem on the front. I walked along staring at my new prized possession, smiling as I went. A voice calling to me, brought me out of my daydream. I scanned the path in front of me, still smiling as I did.

The smile quickly faded from my face. On the path ahead, were two boys sitting on the railings of the bridge that crossed the small river between me and the school. Billy Johnson sat on one side of the bridge and Henry Johnson sat on the other. Billy was the older of the two Johnson boys. Henry was two years his junior and followed whatever his older brother did. I got the feeling that he wouldn't have been all that bad of a kid if it weren't for his older brother egging him on all the time. Henry was looking down at the ground and didn't look up when Billy called out to me again.

"Hey fatty, I'm talking to you," he called to me, from his perch atop the railing.

I kept walking toward the bridge. It was the only way to get to the school, if I was to get there before the bell rang. I was hoping that they would just call me names and then leave me alone.

"Are you hard of hearing or are you just stupid?" Billy yelled at me.

"I don't want any trouble. I'm just trying to get to school," I said, my voice trembling.

"No problem, but if you want to cross the bridge, you'll have to pay the toll," he said.

"I don't have any money," I said, and kept walking.

I was nearly at the bridge now and Billy jumped down from the railing to block my way.

"If you want to pass, you'll have to give Henry there a blowjob," he said, motioning toward his brother.

"Leave him alone, he's just a kid," Henry pleaded.

"Shut the fuck up, or when I'm done beatin' the shit out of fatty here, it'll be your turn!" Billy yelled at his brother.

His face was red, and he was spitting as he yelled. He pumped the fist of his right hand up and down in a hammering motion.

Henry got down slowly from his perch atop the railing of the bridge. When he reached the ground, he stood with his hands in his pockets, staring at the ground.

"I think we should just let him be," he said quietly, kicking at the stones lining the path with his sneaker.

I never saw anyone move so fast in my entire life. Billy took three strides across the path and punched him in the mouth, before he had time to move.

He went sprawling backwards, landing on his back in the grass alongside the path. Blood trickled from his right nostril and from the corner of his mouth. Henry reached up to wipe at the blood. Tears began running down his face and he sniffled from the blood and snot collecting in his nose. He spat a large mixture of blood and saliva onto the path in front of him. He lie there looking up at his brother, a hurt look painted painfully across his face.

"Now look what you made me do. You think I like hitting my younger brother? All you have to do is listen once in a while," Billy said, extending his hand to help him to his feet.

He slowly reached up and grabbed hold of his hand. His right cheek was all red and puffy, but he had stopped crying. He got to his feet and stood looking at the ground again.

I started to walk toward the bridge, but I didn't get more than a couple of feet, before Billy swung in my direction. I stopped in my tracks, not wanting what happened to Henry, to happen to me. He loved his younger brother. I shuddered to think what would happen to me, the fat kid that he didn't like. A shiver ran through me from my head to my feet. I couldn't have moved if I had wanted to. My legs felt like rubber and I was sweating all over. My mouth was dry, and I had to pee really badly. I knew at that point, that this was not going to end well for me.

"Where you going, you fat fuck?" Billy screamed.

"I have to get to school."

"You're not going anywhere, until you pay the fuckin' toll."

"I'm not giving Henry a blowjob," I said, crying now.

"Well then, you'll have to give us something," he said and plucked my new hat from my head, faster than a cat catching a mouse.

"Hey, give me that back," I protested, but I knew it was of no use.

"This is one smart hat. Isn't it, Henry?" he said, while loosening the strap on the back.

"Sure is Billy," he said, eyes still a little downcast.

"This fucking thing is too small. Here you try it," he said, as he threw it to Henry.

He tried it on half-heartedly and then held it out to me. I went to grab for it, but Billy hit my arm down, out of the way.

"It's of no use to us. Go ahead and piss in it, Henry," he said.

He started to grumble about doing what his big brother asked him to do but thought better of it. He threw my prized hat on the ground and pissed in it. There was a large puddle of urine pooled in the upside - down hat.

"Now put your hat back on, you fat fuck!" Billy ordered.

I started to cry again. I knew that if I didn't put the hat on, things were going to get worse for me. I picked up the hat and very hesitantly turned it over so some of the urine poured out of the hat and onto the path at my feet.

"Put it on!" he yelled.

I slowly lifted the hat. Warm urine ran into my hand. I grabbed it from the bill and slowly lowered it onto my head. Urine soaked into my hair and ran down my face and neck. I gagged at the feel of it, at the thought of it.

Billy laughed with delight, clapping his hands together, clearly very satisfied with the outcome. Henry stood off to one side, still looking at the ground.

"Now give me your lunch box. It doesn't look like you need to eat anyway," Billy snarled.

I slowly handed him my lunch box and stood there looking down at the ground, in much the same manner as Henry.

He opened the lunch box to examine its contents. There was a peanut butter and jelly sandwich, an apple, a granola bar and a juice box inside. He took a bite out of the apple and then threw it into the river. He stuck the rest of the stuff in his pockets. He threw my lunch box to the ground and stomped on it with both feet. He jumped up and down on it several times, until it was smashed into a hundred pieces. He looked up at me and smiled crazily, obviously very pleased with himself.

"I don't want no stupid Scooby-Doo lunch box. That's for stupid little kids like you. Now get the fuck out of here, before I beat you to within an inch of your life. And don't be tattlin' on us, or you'll get it worse next time," Billy said.

Tears started to pour down my cheeks, uncontrollably. I turned and ran, sobbing, down the path in the direction that I had come. Billy was laughing hysterically behind me.

"I thought you were going to school?" he called after me, laughing all the while.

I ran as far as I could, sweat and urine running onto my face and into my eyes. I stopped finally to catch my breath and wipe at my stinging eyes.

The day no longer seemed fresh and aromatic. The air felt stinging cold and the scent of the leaves smelled of rot and disgust. My happy mood was replaced with misery and despair. I sobbed uncontrollably. The day had started with me being happier than I could ever remember, and now I couldn't imagine ever feeling worse than I did at that moment.

My parents were at work, which was fine by me. I was humiliated enough, and I didn't need them seeing me in this state. I went home, had a shower and changed my clothes. I washed my hat in the sink as best I could and then dried it with a hair dryer. It was the last time I tried to wear it to school. The hat that I was so proud to show off, never ever made it there. I was too afraid that Billy would steal it or wreck it. I opened the refrigerator and got out the chocolate cake that was left over from supper. I ate it, along with eight cookies and a glass of milk. That made me feel a bit better, but somehow worse at the same time. I sat on the couch for fifteen minutes, just staring at the wall. I couldn't bear the thought of going to school, but I didn't want to get in trouble for skipping. I decided to ride my bike out to see Grandma. She always knew how to cheer me up and I could sure use some cheering up.

I rode slowly, avoiding as many of the main streets as I could, not wanting anyone to see me and tell my parents that I wasn't in school. I still needed time to regroup after the ordeal I had been through. When I got to the retirement home, I found her sitting on a bench in the garden. It's funny how I never knew the name of the retirement home. I was there dozens of times over the years and hadn't paid attention to what the name of it was. Anyway, she was surprised to see me of course and she got up from her bench, when she saw me.

"Aren't you supposed to be in school?" she started to say but realized very quickly when she saw the state that I was in, that something was definitely wrong.

"What's wrong dear?" she asked.

I burst into tears and ran to her, flung my arms around her and held on for dear life. Tears ran down my face again and I sobbed in long retching bursts of tears and snot. She held me tightly, waiting for me to stop. After my sobbing had subsided, she broke the silence.

"There, there sweetheart. Tell your ole Granny what's the matter, so she can make it all better," she said kindly, still holding me.

"I... I... was on my way... on my way to school," I tried to say between breaths.

All the sobbing had left me breathless. My eyes were red and swollen. I looked worse than Henry did after Billy socked him one. She understood; she was very patient and kind.

"Just breathe, everything will be alright. Grandma is here," she said in a soothing voice.

I took a couple of minutes to catch my breath and collect my thoughts, before I tried again. This time when I started, I found that I was able to talk coherently.

"I was on my way to school. I left early because I wanted to show off my new hat that Dad bought me on the weekend. I cut through the woods and followed the path that leads to the bridge. It crosses the river and comes out at the back of the schoolyard. When I got to the bridge there were two older boys there and they wouldn't let me cross the bridge. They wanted me to pay a toll, but I didn't have any money. They peed in my hat and broke my Scooby-Doo lunch box, because I didn't pay the toll," I said, looking down at the ground.

Grandma took a half step back, so that she could see my face. She took my chin gently in her hand and raised it up, so that I was looking her in the eyes. She took a handkerchief out of her pocket and dabbed the tears from the corners of my eyes and then my cheeks.

"I'm sorry you had to go through that sweetheart. Bullies like that will get what's coming to them someday. Do you know what karma is Jacky?" she asked.

"No, I don't."

"Well, let's see if I can explain. Come sit with me," she said, as she turned and headed for the bench.

"Ahh, that's better. Now let me think. Okay, I believe that everything in the universe has a balancing point. Everything evens out. If you do bad deeds, then you will have bad things done to you. If you do good deeds, then good things will happen to you in return. Things have a way of evening themselves out and that's what I call karma. So, when those bullies were mean to you, that means that they will have bad things happen to them in return. Don't be too sad about what happened to you today, because you know that they will pay for it in the end. Do you understand?"

"I think so Grandma. I just wish that everyone could be nice. I don't want bad things to happen to me or anyone else," I said.

"See that's good karma right there. You keep thinking like that and good things will follow you. You can't control the way other people behave, but you certainly can control the way you do. Never waste your time with thoughts of revenge. Karma will take care of that for you. I'm going to tell you something a wise man once told me. Revenge is like swallowing poison and thinking that it will kill your enemies. Do you know what he meant by that?" she asked.

"No, I don't think I do," I said.

"He meant that it only hurts you. If you are consumed by getting revenge, you aren't enjoying your life. Meanwhile your enemies are living their lives, without any thought to how miserable you are. They don't care about you; so why should you care about them? Does that make sense?"

"Yes, I get it now," I said, happily.

"Remember. Others can't make you feel small or unimportant, only you can do that. What others think of you has absolutely nothing to do with you," she said emphatically.

"I hope that helps and I hope you feel better. You definitely look better. They should still be serving breakfast. Come, walk with your old Granny, up to get something to eat."

"Okay Grandma, and thanks. I do feel much better. I always do, after talking to you. I love you Grandma," I said, and then threw my arms around her and gave her as tight a hug as I could muster.

"I love you too sweetheart. I'll tell you a little secret, just between you and me. You were always my favourite," she said and kissed me on the cheek.

I was beaming with pride. My smile went from ear to ear and I felt on top of the world once again.

I spent the next few hours talking with Grandma. She told me some stories about when she was a child and about Dad as a child. She was always a great story teller.

I hadn't thought about that day that I had spent with her in many years. The next time Billy tried to bully me, it didn't work. He could tell that I wasn't bothered by him any longer and so he moved on to someone else. Sometime over the next while however, I forgot to heed the advice that she had given me on that day. The bullying started to affect me negatively again. It took me until just this moment, that I remembered what she told me on that visit. Boy oh boy, do I miss her.

CHAPTER SIX

I spent the week with my sister's family and we had fun camping, swimming and fishing. The first few days I had a lot of fun, especially with Nate and Brian. The latter part of the week was a different story. I felt like I was spinning my wheels. I wanted to get home and start trying to get my life in order. How exactly I was going to do that, remained a mystery, but I was anxious to get home nevertheless. Contacting Vicki again was out of the question. She had made it abundantly clear, that she needed some space and I was going to respect her wishes. It wouldn't be easy, but I knew that if I had any hope of a lasting relationship with her, I had to try.

When I got home from my camping trip I decided that I was going to have to deal with bad Jack. Pretending that he didn't exist wasn't the answer any longer. I was going to have to be more proactive. First, I had to go through all of Grandma's stuff. I had a huge file at home that I had brought back with me from her house. She kept a detailed diary of very useful information pertaining to the subject of travelling. There was also a lot of information about bad Jack. She had always kept a close eye on him over the years. That brought me to my second order of business. I was going to do some reconnaissance of my own. I needed to know more about him and his world.

I went to the basement and got out her large folder. The file was nearly four inches thick. It was more like a large envelope, I guess. There was a flap that overlapped and was held in place with a red string that was wrapped around a catch on the front. I had opened it once before, but only briefly. This time I was going to be more methodical and read every last scrap of paper. It was filled with news clippings, photographs, letters and notes. Some were official looking and some were written on napkins and scraps of paper.

It was the note on the very top that caught my attention. Her penmanship was beautiful. I recognized it right away, as the same writing that graced the inside of every birthday card, that I ever got from her. It was addressed: To my Dearest Jacky.

It read as follows:

I've compiled this folder full of information, that I'm sure you will find very useful. If you're reading this, then I must be dead and gone. Not to worry; maybe we'll meet in another world or another time. I love you Jacky; you were always my favourite.

I know I've said it so many times that you must be getting sick of hearing it by now, but you must be careful of bad Jack. His Grandma was pure evil, and I think he may just be a chip off the old block. Be sure to read everything carefully. There's good information here to help you fit in, when you travel. I've also left a contact number for Dr. Bruce Rolles. He is the Professor of Anthropology at the University here on the other side. Go see him. You'll like him.

Love Grandma.

I did just as she bid of me. I left the file to read for another day and I went to see Dr. Rolles at the university.

The university was right in the centre of town. It was an imposing structure made entirely of stone. Ivy covered the walls that faced to the south, softening the look slightly. There were two twin towers at either end of the building. The east one held a large clock that looked as if its edges and hands were made of polished brass. The west tower held a large bell that appeared as though it too, was made of brass. The roof was copper that had oxidized and turned green, except for one ten - foot square area that had recently been replaced and was still copper colour. The bell began to ring as I was still looking up. A slow, steady chime that I could feel as well as hear. It was so loud that a group of children covered their ears as they passed by on the sidewalk beside me. It rang out twelve times, marking the noon hour and then fell silent again, save for the echoes bouncing in the commons.

The walk up to the main entrance was covered with interlocking brick and lined with trees. The canopies of the trees overlapped each other, making what looked like a covered bridge. I had seen but one covered bridge in my lifetime, the time my parents took Helen and me out east on summer vacation. This reminded me of that bridge. I followed the walkway up to the massive wooden doors that formed the main entrance to the University. I knew this because it said: Main Entrance, on a sign posted on the wall to the right of the doors. The doors glided open on their hinges without any resistance. I was expecting the doors to be stubborn because of their size and so, I pulled far too hard. The door swung open quickly and struck the railing on the side of the step with a dull thud that echoed in the hallway. A good number of students and staff shot me a disapproving look, before continuing on their way. I closed the door gently behind me and continued down the hall to the main office.

There was one person in line ahead of me. He was a short fellow with a squeaky voice and he seemed to be a little upset about something. I didn't want to eavesdrop, so I kept my distance. He gave up trying to accomplish whatever it was that he set out to, and stormed off, muttering under his breath as he went.

I approached the counter slowly, expecting the receptionist to be in a foul mood, after her last encounter. I was greeted with a very warm, genuine smile.

"Good morning. How can I help you?" Melissa said, from behind the counter.

"I need to speak with Dr. Rolles, professor of Anthropology," I said.

"Yeah, I know Dr. Rolles, everyone knows Dr. Rolles. Do you have an appointment?"

"No, I'm sorry I don't. Do I need one?" I asked.

"No need to apologize. He's a pretty popular guy around here, so an appointment is usually necessary. I'll just buzz him and see if he's available, okay? Who should I say is calling?"

"Oh, tell him that it's Jack Armstrong. Betty Armstrong's grandson. If you please," I said hesitantly.

I was hoping that Grandma's name might carry some weight with the professor. There was no way of knowing for sure, whether he even knew her though.

Melissa rang the professor's room and he picked up on the second ring. I could hear him answer from where I was standing, on the other side of the counter. Melissa held the phone out from her ear and mouthed the word "wow" to me.

"I have a Jack Armstrong here to see you. He says that he is Betty Armstrong's grandson."

"Yes, I know who he is. Send him right up. I'll clear my schedule," the professor said with no attempt to hide the excitement in his voice.

Melissa held the phone out farther from her ear and put the tip of her finger in it. She hung up the phone and took a few seconds to wiggle her ear a bit, before talking.

"So, I guess you probably heard what the good Doctor said. He's quite the character, and boy is he loud and excitable. You'll like him. Everyone does. His enthusiasm is infectious. Here, I'll draw you a map. I'm assuming this is the first time to the university, based on your entrance earlier," she said, with a laugh.

"Yeah, sorry about that," I said sheepishly.

"No need to apologize, just yankin' your chain a little, that's all. Anyway, here are the directions," she said, and handed me the map.

The map was of the third floor and was easy enough to follow, but I didn't know how to get to the third floor. I must have had a puzzled look on my face, because when I looked up, Melissa was pointing down the hall. I followed the direction she was pointing with my eyes and saw a sign that clearly marked the elevator.

"Thank you, Melissa," I said, and walked toward it.

"You're welcome Jack, anytime."

The elevator whisked me up to the third floor so fast that when it stopped, it felt as though I was floating for a moment. The doors slid open and I stepped into the hallway. The floors were polished smooth like you would see in a museum. They appeared to be made of granite. The walls were still the same solid stone construction. No attempt was made to soften them or to dress them up in any way. There were pictures on the walls of various archaeological sites and animals however.

I followed the directions until I came upon a bright orange door at the end of the hallway. The door contrasted completely with the drabness of the walls and the black and white speckled flooring. I found out pretty quickly, that the colour of the door was certainly no accident. It was a beacon in the darkness, as was the man behind the door.

I knocked loudly on the door and waited. I could hear someone stirring inside. The sound of papers being shuffled and the sound of someone muttering to himself was unmistakable. I knocked again, in case he didn't hear me above all the noise he was making inside.

"Keep your pants on. I'm coming," a booming, and somewhat intimidating voice said, from the other side of the door.

I took a couple of steps back and waited patiently. The sound of shuffling papers continued, and the muttering intensified. Finally, the noise subsided, and the unmistakable sound of footsteps approached the door. The door opened with a swoosh of air, sending papers from a nearby desk flying to the floor in all directions. The little man that had opened the door went scurrying to pick them up, muttering to himself as he went. I stood at the door, waiting until he was done retrieving the papers.

"Don't just stand there, help me!" he said, in his booming voice.

I stood motionless for several seconds, trying to process just what was going on. It threw me off guard to hear such a commanding voice come from such a small person. The good doctor, if that's who this was, stood less than five feet tall, and looked to be less than a hundred pounds, soaking wet. He had grey hair that was white at the temples. It stood on end as though he was experiencing a bad case of static cling. He was dressed in blue jeans and a white dress shirt with tufts at the wrists and a purple vest. A large pocket watch hung from a large gold chain around his neck. He wore black, thick rimmed glasses that sat slightly askew at the present.

"Never mind, I've just about got them now!" he said.

I was still standing at the door. I had been so enthralled with the scene playing out in front of me, that I neglected to help him as he had asked. I was worried that we might have gotten off on the wrong foot and that he might not be willing to help me after all.

"I'm so sorry. I don't know what's gotten into me," I apologized.

"No need to apologize. I seem to have that effect on people. I don't think that they expect my voice coming from, well, me," he said, as he ran his hands through the air motioning from the floor to above his head.

He combed his hair flat with the palms of his hands, but immediately hairs started to free themselves and stick out again. He held his hand out to me and smiled the biggest smile I had ever seen.

"I'm Professor Bruce Rolles, at your service," he said, shaking my hand with both of his.

He paused for a minute, looking me up and down from head to foot.

"So, Betty was your Grandma. I can see the resemblance; I can definitely see the resemblance. She was quite the looker in her day, too bad she went for the tall ones like your grandpa and not short guys like me. She was a free thinker, brilliant..., brilliant like me, I would say. There are many who would agree with both statements, I would say," the Professor said.

"You don't say," I teased. I couldn't resist.

"I would say... and that's why I said it."

I couldn't tell if he was playing along, or if he was just oblivious to his repetition of 'I would say'.

"We have lots to talk about, I would say. Yes, lots to talk about. We should go into my study where we can get more comfortable and get better acquainted. I've cleared my schedule so that we won't be interrupted."

I guess that he was just oblivious, after all.

I followed him across the room. It was a large open hall, more than it was a room. The ceilings were twenty feet high and the walls were covered with book shelves. There wasn't an empty spot on any of them. There were large tables set up in rows. The rows were four tables wide and ten tables deep. At each table, there were four chairs and a large computer screen. There was a large table with one chair at the front of the hall. I assumed that it must be his desk, at the front, of what looked like his classroom. There were stacks of papers piled neatly on either end of his desk and on top of each pile was a signed photograph. The one to the left was of Henry Ford and the one on the right was of Albert Einstein. This contrasted the desks near the door, that were also piled high with papers, but were in total disarray.

"Ah, welcome to my home away from home, although I suppose that I spend more time here than there. A lot of great thinkers have passed through these doors, I would say."

He must have noticed that I was very interested in his classroom, and that I had fallen behind him.

"A very interesting classroom, I would say."

Now he had me saying it. He was infectious that was for sure. Time would tell, if that was a good thing or a bad thing.

I followed him into his study. This room was smaller than the hall we had just come from. I would go as far as saying it was actually quite cozy. The walls were again covered in book cases that were also filled with books. There was a small desk and chair against the far wall. This desk was completely clear except for a couple of picture frames, one at either end of the desk. In the corner was a recliner with a light above it and a small sofa facing it. It was to this corner that he led me. He sat in the recliner and he motioned for me to sit on the sofa.

"Make yourself at home my boy. Do you want anything to drink?" he asked cheerily.

"No, I'm fine thank you."

"Well, if you do want anything, just help yourself to the fridge there," he said, pointing over my shoulder to the other corner of the room.

"Okay. I could guess what brings you by, but I'd rather hear it from you. It might be the only time you get to talk. I've been told, I tend to ramble," he said with a laugh.

I had just met him, but he did strike me as the type of fellow that could monopolize a conversation.

"I found a note in a folder of my Grandma's. She thought that it would be a good idea if we met. So, here I am."

"Yes, here you are. Where exactly is here. Have you ever given it much thought?" he asked.

I wasn't entirely sure what he was referring to, but I took a stab at it anyway.

"From my point of view, this place is some sort of alternate world. It looks the same as my world in most ways. When I look up at the sky I can see the same stars and moon as where I'm from. To be honest, I've never really wrapped my head around, how it's all possible. I've just learned to accept it and I stopped questioning it."

"Ahh, I see. This place is the other Earth, as far as you're concerned. Where you live is the real Earth. People from here would have a different point of view, I would say. Of course, everyone's point of view is all relative. It depends on what side of the fence you are on, I would say."

"I would definitely agree with that statement," I said.

"Let me ask you a question. If there were two worlds, call them your Earth and my Earth; would you expect that the sky would look the same to you on both of them?" he asked.

"No, I would expect that they'd be different somehow. I would be seeing it from a different angle."

"And do you think that you would notice that subtle change from one to the other?" he asked.

I could tell that he was just having fun with me. I was certain that he had asked these same questions, to many people before me.

"I'm not sure. That's why I gave up trying to figure it out long ago. All I know is that the two worlds exist, and I accepted that fact, and moved on," I said, rather matter of factly.

"If there were two separate worlds, would you not be able to see it, and they you. Is one world invisible to the other, but there are two worlds rotating around the same sun?" he asked, smiling as he did.

"I'm not sure," I said, flatly.

"My colleagues and I have given it much thought over the years. We have also tested many theories and there is only one that truly fits. This earth and the other exist in the same place and time. Everything is exactly the same. They are orbiting the sun the same, and all the physical characteristics are the same because they are not separate entities. That is to say, that there aren't two of them per se.

There is one space that they both occupy. From our point of view, there are two worlds or realities, but from the planet's perspective there is only one planet," he finished, with a long exhale, followed by a deep breath.

"Does that make sense to you?" he asked.

"I would say yes and no. No, you know what; none of it makes sense and that's why I stopped trying to figure it out. I just know that there is a world separate from mine, that I can go visit. I'm okay with leaving it that," I said.

"Well, if you're okay with leaving it at that, then I suppose I will leave it at that. You did come to see me for some reason and I'm guessing it wasn't just because your Grandma told you to. Why did you come to see me Jack?" he asked, leaning forward in his recliner.

I could tell that this was his favourite topic in the whole world, and he was a little put off that I didn't want to pursue it any further. He still had hopes it seemed, that I could be of interest to him yet.

"I was wondering if you could help me, to understand the relationship between me and my twin in this world. Is there any way, that I can stop him from bothering me? That kind of thing."

The professor clapped his hands together and then brought them up in front of his face. His eyes were sparkling out from behind them. He made some little giggling noises and then removed his hands to reveal an enormous grin.

"It would be my absolute pleasure to help you in that regard. Adventure is my middle name. Well actually no, it is in fact Henry, but the point is, I live for adventure... and discovery. I would be thrilled to death. Well, actually no, I wouldn't be thrilled to die. My point is, that I would be very excited to help you, I would say."

"Okay, where do we start?"

"It's not where we start, it's where you start. Go home and finish looking through the folder that your Grandma made for you, then come back and see me. We'll be on the same page then. It's been a while since I have seen what she put in her folder, but I do remember most of it, I would say. Bring it with you when you come back, and we can go over it together. Is tomorrow okay with you? I'm anxious to get the ball rolling. Tomorrow should be fine, should be fine, I would say."

He struck me as the kind of person who could have a conversation with someone or with himself, and he really was fine with it either way.

"Tomorrow would be fine, I guess. What time would be good for you?"

"Any time is fine by me, I would say. Although morning would be better. It would give us a chance to go over your folder and talk things over."

"It's a date then. I'll be here at nine. I'm going to go home right now and go through the folder. I very much want to get things figured out as soon as possible."

We shook hands and I let myself out, while he lit up his pipe and relaxed in his recliner. I marvelled again at the sheer size of the hall outside his study. I noticed now that the tops of the book cases were all intricately carved, with all types of mythical creatures. Very cool indeed.

I waved to Melissa on the way out. She smiled pleasantly and motioned for me to come over.

"So, what did you think of the professor?" she asked.

"I liked him. A bit eccentric, I would say," I said laughing.

She thought that was uproariously funny and laughed until she cried. When she had stopped laughing, she wiped the tears from her eyes and said:

"You noticed that I see. He sure does say that a lot, doesn't he?"

"He sure does. I think it's kinda funny. It definitely adds to his quirkiness, his likeability."

"Yeah, like I said before. Everyone around these parts knows the professor."

"Well, I guess I'll be seeing you tomorrow Melissa. I've scheduled another meeting with the professor for tomorrow at nine."

"All righty then. I'll see you tomorrow. The doors will be open at eight thirty. I'll be here," she said, smiling and blushing a little.

"See you then."

CHAPTER SEVEN

Grandma had filled the folder with all kinds of information about the politics and laws of the other world. Many were the same and even some of the politicians looked familiar. There were interesting articles about the economy. A lot of pictures with descriptions of the town that mirrored my own. I looked through the folder for a couple of hours before taking a break. All that reading made me tired and I lie down for a nap. I awoke refreshed and ready to tackle the folder again. I waded through pages and pages of pictures. Most of them were of bad Jack and his family. I found it a little disturbing frankly, how much time she spent spying on him and his family. There were articles from the local paper that she had cut out and pasted to a page in a circle around the outside. In the middle was a mug shot of bad Jack. The articles were from the police blotter in the newspaper. There were nine entries in all. None of them were serious in nature. There were a couple of break and enters, a couple of assaults, some fraud charges and some petty theft charges. There was one however, that made the hair on the back of my neck stand on end. This particular article was folded several times so that it would fit onto the page. I could still see the headline. Grandma had taken care to fold the newspaper article in such a way that the headline could be read.

The newspaper article read as follows:

Local man charged in a string of sexual assaults, spanning the last three years.

Jack Armstrong appeared in court for the first time on Monday, to answer to fifteen charges of sexual assault. Jack Armstrong of 21 Haven crescent, has been in custody since December 24. Local police had received complaints from seventeen local women spanning three years. On several occasions 911 dispatch was contacted, but when police arrived, the assailant had fled the scene. The police had been warning the community that there was a sexual predator in our neighbourhood, but they were never able to obtain a reliable description of the man in question. The police had devoted two of its detectives to the case, for the past two plus years. A break came in the case six months ago, when one of the women was able to provide a partial description of the assailant. Up to that point, he had been careful to hide his face with a mask. The woman that can't be named for confidentiality reasons, was able to fight off her attacker and in the process, rip off his mask. The mask was examined for DNA matches in the system data base.

The data base logs fingerprints and DNA samples from convicted felons. In this case, the samples taken from the mask matched that of Jack Michael Armstrong of 21 Haven crescent. He had a long list of trouble with the law. The Focus Newspaper, tried to contact his parents at that address, but they were unavailable for comment.

The judge that presided over the case was unavailable for comment, but a prepared statement from the court was read at a press conference this afternoon at the courthouse. It read as follows:

Jack Michael Armstrong was arraigned on fifteen charges of sexual assault and earlier today appeared in court number one, of the criminal division with honourable James Belding presiding. Judge Belding cited inconsistencies and improper search and recovery of evidence, as reasons for the dismissal of all charges against Jack Michael Armstrong.

A statement from the local police was attached to this document and read as follows:

Your local police department takes our community safety very seriously and strive to do our utmost to earn your trust and protect our citizens. We would like to take this opportunity to apologize to the women and their families affected by this case. We will endeavour to continue to protect our community in the professional manner that you have become accustomed to. We are in the process of developing new policies to ensure that egregious miscarriages of justice such as these, are a thing of the past.

I couldn't believe what I was reading. Firstly, the news about him being a serial rapist, and secondly, the handling of the case by the police department. The police department in my world, would never have written a statement like that. It was a toss-up as to which part shocked me more.

The mug shot in the centre of the page made my skin crawl. When I first glanced at it, I didn't give it much thought. After I had finished reading the articles and saw what he had been charged with; it gave me a whole new sense of what a monster he was. In the picture, his hair was long and greasy, and his face was scruffy. It wasn't quite a beard yet, but it was several days' growth to be sure. It wasn't so much his unpleasant, unkempt look that disturbed me. It was his eyes and his smile that were disconcerting. His eyes sparkled with delight and his mouth formed a twisted grin.

There was something terrifyingly familiar about that twisted grin. It took me a few seconds to figure it out, but it all came rushing back to me and I felt a shiver run up and down my spine. It was the same twisted grin that the other Grandma had shown me, that day long ago at the retirement home.

I turned the page over so that I didn't have to look at the picture any longer. I paused for a moment, trying to collect myself, before moving on to the rest of the folder. I was about two thirds of the way through the folder now, and to be honest, I couldn't wait to be done. At the beginning, it was an interesting journey of discovery. Now it had become an arduous task, that I wanted to be done with as soon as possible.

I pushed myself to continue. There were interesting newspaper articles that gave me a little history lesson about the town. My recollection of the history of my own town wasn't very good, so I wasn't sure if it differed from my own or not. Apparently, this town was a jumping off point for the Underground Railroad, because of its proximity to the border. There were pictures of some of the families that had escaped slavery and headed into Canada. There were also many pictures of some of the families that helped the slaves realize their dreams of being free.

Under one such picture, in Grandma's beautiful scrawling cursive was written: This picture was taken in front of the family home. Our relatives were instrumental in helping many families break free from slavery.

I was very proud to learn that my family was involved in the Underground Railway, but I was confused at the same time. Every article or picture I had found up to this point had been about the twin town. Why she had included a picture from my home town, was a bit of a mystery.

She included local bylaws and other laws that were different there than here. Most were just subtle changes that didn't amount to any difference at all. I didn't bother to read all of it. I just skimmed through it and would come back to it later, when I had more time.

There were lots of historical pictures of the town, showing what the town looked like, then and now. There were more newspaper articles, pictures and notes. I flipped the pages quickly, glancing at them slightly as I did. My interest was fading fast and I just wanted to be done. Unless there was something really interesting that caught my eye. I was just going to get to the end of the folder and call it done.

Underneath all the photos, newspaper articles, notes and letters, was one last item that caught my attention. It was a birth certificate and baby picture of bad Jack. There was a newspaper clipping of the announcement of Jack Henry Armstrong and along with it all the particulars of his birth. Nothing out of the ordinary there. Attached to this article was a letter addressed to me. It read as follows:

My dearest Jack. I love you more than you will ever know. I'm not sorry for what I've done, but I am truly sorry that you have to find out this way. I should have had the courage to tell you this face to face. I always thought that there would be a right time, and so I continued to put it off, until sadly I have run out of time. I have always made it clear to you that bad Jack was a bad seed. What I never told you was that I could see this from the time he was an infant. If you are reading this, then you are no doubt holding in your hand, a baby picture and birth certificate of Jack Henry Armstrong. These do not belong to him. They belong to you. I knew early on that he was a bad seed and so I switched the two of you when you were infants. You were born in the hospital in the other town and he was born here. I'm sure this must be very hard for you to hear and I'm sorry from the bottom of my heart. I felt that it was the right decision then and I stand by that decision to this day. I'm sorry for any pain that this may cause you and I hope that you can forgive me for what I have done. I had only your best interests in mind.

Love Grandma.

I stared at the note for a long time, unable to fully grasp what I had just seen. I read the note over again, carefully. I looked at the picture and birth certificate in my hand and then back to the note. I read the note once more, before closing the folder and lying it on the coffee table. I set the picture and the birth certificate on top of the folder, along with the note from my Grandma. I sat for a minute staring off into nothing. My thoughts were an incoherent mess. I went to the kitchen and grabbed a beer from the refrigerator. I am not a big drinker, but I drank the beer in one swig and then opened another. I went back and slouched down on the sofa and stared at the closed folder with the note on top. I was numb, unable to form a complete thought. I wasn't sure I wanted to think about what it all meant. Eventually though, my mind started to mull it over, despite my protestations. My mind needed to make sense of it, even though I wanted nothing more than to just drink myself into oblivion.

I finished my second beer and opened a third. I drank it and then turned on the television. I sat staring at the screen. There was a news reporter talking about an earthquake somewhere. That was about as far as I got before my beer was empty and I needed a refill. I got a beer then another and then went back to the living room and sprawled out on the couch again.

I awoke to the sound of someone knocking on the door. I rolled over on to my face to shield my eyes from the brightness of the room. The knocking continued, only now it was accompanied by a pounding in my head as well. With every knock at the door, there was a throbbing in my head, that sent little bursts of light to the back of my closed eyes. I ignored the sound, hoping that it would go away. The knocking continued. It was apparent, that whoever was at the door wasn't going away. I got up and staggered to the door. It felt as though something had crawled inside my mouth and died, while I was asleep. I ran my tongue along the outside of my teeth and swallowed hard a couple of times. The bad taste in my mouth persisted, and so did the knocking at the door. I made my way slowly to the door and opened it. I shielded my eyes from the bright light of the mid-morning sun.

There, standing on my front step was the professor. He was wearing a black trench coat and dark sunglasses. His hair was sticking up in all directions. He ran his hands over the sides of it, from front to back, but it immediately started to stick out again.

"Someone has had a hard night, I would say."

"Humph," is what came out, when I tried to respond.

"May I come in?" he asked.

"Suit yourself," I said, as I turned and walked back to the couch and sat down.

I sat with my face in my hands, eyes closed, hoping that my head would stop throbbing. At least the knocking on the door had stopped. I heard the door close, and the professor came into the living room and sat in the chair facing me.

"I thought we were going to meet in your study?" I managed.

"Yes, that's right. We were to meet at nine o'clock this morning. It is now ten after eleven and I was concerned that something had happened to you; so here I am."

"It's that late? I must have slept in. Sorry."

"No need to apologize. From the looks of it, you had a few too many beers last night," he said, pointing at all the empty bottles strewn across the coffee table.

"Could you excuse me for one second please?" I asked, as I got up and went to the bathroom.

The professor didn't say anything, he just nodded in agreement.

I went into the bathroom and closed the door. I ran the cold water from the faucet while I searched the medicine cabinet for some pain pills. I shook two pills into my palm and swallowed them with a mouthful of water. I stuck my head under the cold water and left it there for several minutes. The cold water helped, or the drugs started to kick in. Either way, I felt better than I did a few minutes ago. I dried my hair with a towel and brushed my teeth. When I left the bathroom and went back out to the living room, I felt almost human again.

"Sorry to keep you waiting, had a hard time waking up this morning."

"I can see that. What's the occasion?"

"I can see that you are a traveller as well," I said, ignoring his question.

"If by traveller you mean that I can pass between the two worlds; then yes, I am most certainly a traveller. A very special type of traveller, I would say."

"What do you mean, when you say, a special type of traveller?"

"I'm not sure how much you know about travellers, as you call us. I'm guessing your Grandma filled you in on most of the important stuff. I am different because I have an identical twin that is also a traveller. So, there are in fact four of us. Now, because we are twins we are not opposites of our brethren from the other world. We are in fact, remarkably similar. We have all been able to travel from infancy, which as you can imagine, gave our parents fits. Unlike other travellers' counterparts, we actually maintain a relationship with one another and so did our parents. You should see us when we all get together, it's a hoot."

"That's amazing. I can imagine that it must be something to see you all together," I said, shaking my head and laughing.

"I imagine that before we are done here, you will see the rest of us. Now, what did you learn from the folder that she left for you? I knew that she was preparing one for you, but I never got to see it, completed."

"There was a lot of information to help me navigate your world. Laws and politics and things like that. There was of course a lot of information on bad Jack. Some very shocking information."

"That's a very apt name, you have given him. He is bad through and through. I would say," he said, sighing.

"So, I'm guessing you didn't know about Grandma's little switcheroo?" I asked.

"I'm sorry, I don't follow you," he said, his eyes narrowing.

"I guess that answers that question," I said, and handed him the letter from her.

He took the letter and began to read. I watched his face. His expression started out neutral but as he continued to read, his brow furrowed, and he began to stroke his chin with his left hand. I could see the concern on his face.

He finished reading the letter and slowly handed it back to me. He looked sad. His eyes were no longer twinkling, and the look of concern remained, across his face.

"I guess that explains all of this," he said, motioning towards the empty beer bottles on the coffee table.

"I'm sorry Jack. I never knew. This must be a lot for you to process. We can meet later, or tomorrow if you'd like. Give yourself some time to get this straight in your head," he said, kindly.

"That sounds like a good idea. I think I could use some time to figure out where my head is at. Thanks," I said and extended my hand for him to shake.

He brushed past my outstretched hand and gave me a tight and long hug. Under different circumstances, it may have felt strange, but at the time it felt completely right. I hugged him back tightly for several seconds, before letting him go.

"If you need anything, just call me," he said, gave me his business card and left.

It occurred to me after it was too late that I had no way of calling him in the other world, but I stuffed his card into my wallet anyway.

I was left to my thoughts. I was already second guessing telling the professor that I needed to be alone for a while.

I went into the living room and cleaned up the beer bottles and put them in the box by the stove. I sat at the kitchen table staring at the clock hanging on the wall across from me. I thought about calling Vicki, but quickly dismissed the idea. I did the next best thing. I called Helen.

I had plenty of time to go over it in my mind, again and again. I had been doing nothing but that since I had found out that I was switched at birth.

Helen let herself in like she usually did. I was sitting on the couch with my head in my hands.

"What's up big brother? From the looks of it, you've had better days," she asked, sitting beside me and putting her arm around me.

I handed her the letter from Grandma, without looking up. She took it and began to read. She rubbed her hand and arm back and forth across my back as she read. She read it very slowly or she read it more than once. In any case, it was a long while before she spoke.

"Jack, you are one lucky son of a bitch," she said.

I was completely taken aback by what she said. I was expecting some clichés or words of comfort. I wasn't expecting that.

"How in the hell can you read that and say that I'm lucky?" I asked.

"Easy. We can't choose who our family is in this life, and from what you've told me about bad Jack's family; you sure are lucky that she rescued you from that hellish existence. Not to mention gaining me as a sister," she said, smiling and squeezing my shoulder.

"How can you be so cavalier about this? This changes everything."

"This changes nothing! I'm still your sister! Mom and Dad are still your parents! The other Jack is you twin, right? So, you could have just as easily been born here. There's no difference. So, Grandma had to make a small adjustment. No big deal! Get over yourself! Nothing has changed! Except you are starting to become a bit of a whiner in your old age."

"I guess you're right. It's just a lot to process. That's all."

"I can only imagine. I'm serious though. It really doesn't change anything, if you think about it. Well, I guess it does kind of. It's like I said before. Thank your lucky stars, that she did what she did. Otherwise you would have grown up in their family, instead of ours."

"I know you're right, but I still need some time to come to terms with it."

"It'll take a while, but in the meantime, you still have me. I have a few hours before I have to be back. What do you want to do?"

"What would you say to popcorn and a movie?"

"Sounds good to me. You pick the movie and I'll make the popcorn," she said.

Helen and I spent the next two hours cuddled on the couch watching one of our favourite movies. It reminded me of rainy days on the weekends, when we were kids. We would spend hours cuddled on the couch underneath the warmth of Mom's Afghan blanket, watching movies and munching on popcorn.

CHAPTER EIGHT

I knew Helen was right, but it still felt like there was an empty hole inside of me, that had been ripped opened. I needed to fill that hole, before I could move on. I decided to go see my real parents. I knew it was probably not a good idea, to just go strolling up to their door and introduce myself as their real son from another world. It likely wouldn't sit well with bad Jack either. I decided to go see them from a distance, spy on them if you will.

It was early morning, the next morning as a matter of fact. No time to waste. I wanted to move on with my life, but things kept getting thrown in my way, slowing me down, changing my course and making me take detours. I wanted to stake out their house and follow one of them to work. I wore as good a disguise as I could muster on short notice. I had a long black wig left over from some long - ago Halloween party that Vicki and I had attended at one of her cousin's house. I attached a moustache and added some glasses as well. The result was pretty convincing, actually. Someone would have to get close, to tell that it was me. I didn't intend on getting that close to anyone that knew me.

I arrived at their house at 6:30 A.M. and waited just up the street. It was easy to find, thanks to Grandma. There happened to be a bus shelter four or five houses down, on the other side of the street, so I sat there. As I sat and waited, it occurred to me that I was an idiot. It may be possible to catch a glimpse of them as they left the house, but I wasn't going to be able to follow them. What was I going to do? Run after them. In my haste to get things moving and find a decent disguise, I never really thought it through. I did wait so that I could see them emerge from their house and get a bit of a look at them.

She came out first. She was wearing a gaudy brown and orange uniform. Her shirt was short - sleeved and her skirt was hiked above her knees. She was wearing high heels and I could see her make-up from my vantage point, across and down the street. Subtlety was evidently not her strong point. My Mom, my real Mom, wouldn't be caught dead wearing that uniform or with that much make-up on. I watched her drive away and settled in to watch for him.

He came out about forty-five minutes later. He was wearing a nicely tailored, navy blue suit and shiny black dress shoes. He was slimmer than my Dad. He was wearing a pink tie with a gold tie clip. His hair was slicked back with some sort of hair product that made his hair appear wet. He got into his car and sat there for an extended period of time. I was beginning to think that he had spotted me and that's why he hadn't moved. My paranoia turned out to be unfounded after all. A car pulled up out front, and a young attractive blonde got out of a small red sports car. She took a quick look around and then got into the passenger seat of his car. They talked for a while before she left and went back to her car. She sat there and waited until he pulled out and drove down the road past me, and she slowly followed behind. I did my best to stay in the shadow of the bus shelter. It was probably an unnecessary precaution, but I was new to the spy game, and paranoid as hell. It appeared as though he had other things on his mind anyway.

I decided to try and find where the Mother went. It seemed to me, that the Father wasn't going to work today anyway. It appeared, that he was on his way to a meeting of a different kind.

I caught the bus and rode it until I arrived in the downtown core. I found an internet café where I could do some research. I looked up her name, and after several dead ends, found the lead I was searching for. She worked at a small restaurant a couple of blocks away. I took a note pad out of my pocket and quickly scribbled the address with a pen that I bummed from a nerdy looking fellow sitting in a booth next to me. While I was there, I decided to find his information for future reference. He was easier to find. It turns out that he was the C.E.O. of a large sporting goods store chain. There were several articles tying him to bad Jack and the blemish that it had created on his professional and personal life. I jotted down the pertinent information and gave the fellow his pen back.

I walked the couple of blocks over to the restaurant where his Mom was working. Christine's was the name of the place. I walked slowly up to the front window and paused for a minute, leaning against the wall. I looked over my shoulder, trying to look casual. There were two waitresses waiting on customers, but I didn't see his Mom. Perhaps she wasn't a waitress, maybe she worked as a cook. I was too busy trying to see behind the counter, where the cooks were scrambling to satisfy a bustling breakfast crowd. I barely noticed the front door swing open and the woman step out onto the sidewalk beside me. She walked toward me and took up position beside me.

"Do you have a light? I forgot my God damned lighter in my car and it's parked around the block," she said.

I jumped at the sound of her voice. I noticed that someone had come out of the restaurant, not knowing that that someone was standing right beside me. I sure as hell didn't realize that it was bad Jack's Mom. I was standing face to face with a woman, that from a distance looked a little like my own Mother. Now that I saw her up close there was no real resemblance at all. This woman was more tired looking and weathered than my Mom. She appeared defeated and drained, not vibrant like my Mom. She smelled of tobacco and alcohol and her teeth were yellowed from years of smoking.

"You have a light?" she repeated.

"No sorry, don't smoke," I said in a muffled voice, making sure not to make eye contact.

My heart was racing. I was positive that she would think that I was bad Jack. My fears turned out to be unwarranted however. She paid me no notice. She was too busy rummaging through her purse trying to find a lighter or matches, to pay me much attention.

"I know I had some fuckin' matches in this God damned purse of mine. Now, where the hell are they?" she said to herself.

This woman could never be mistaken for my Mom. My Mom was the sweetest person I had ever met. I had never heard her swear in my life, let alone use the Lord's name in vain. This woman seemed pretty rough around the edges, to say the least.

Finally, she found what she was looking for. She produced a booklet of matches with three left in it and held them up triumphantly.

"I knew there were some in here somewhere," she said.

She struck one of the matches and held it to her cigarette. She inhaled deeply and exhaled loudly, with great satisfaction. Moments later she was doubled over at the waste coughing. They came in great retching fits that rattled deep in her chest. The sound was like phlegm and razor blades. I turned my head and tried to put the sound out of my mind. I had to concentrate to not gag at the horrible sound coming from her.

"One of these days these things are going to kill me. Probably be better off I guess, when that day finally comes," she said.

I said nothing. I should have turned and walked away while she was preoccupied trying to find her matches. Now I was stuck. I thought about just turning and walking away but she decided at that moment to strike up a conversation.

"So, you aren't a smoker, and you aren't hungry, or you'd be in there having breakfast. You lookin' for a date?" she asked.

"I might be a little older than you'd like, but I could give you a good deal.

Maybe just go around the corner there, into the alley," she said, winking at me.

That got my legs moving.

"Sorry. You have me confused with someone else. I have to go," I said, as I turned and walked hastily in the other direction, up the street and around the corner.

When I was safely out of sight, I slumped against the wall and slid down to the sidewalk. I was mortified by my encounter with his Mom, or more accurately my birth Mom. Yuck. I shivered at the thought of it. I was sure starting to believe that Helen was right. Grandma did me a huge favour by switching me at birth, but I still wanted to see what my birth Father was like. I had a pretty good idea, that he wasn't a stand-up guy either, based on what I had observed earlier. I still wanted to see for myself, just to tie up any and all loose ends.

I decided to just hang out for a couple of hours at the park down the street. My plan was to burn some time and then go to the office tower where bad Jack's Dad worked. I figured that he might check in at some point during the day. I felt confident that he wouldn't recognize me, based on the encounter I had had earlier with his wife. The thought of it sent a shiver up my spine.

I sat on a bench close to the water. There was a young boy with his mother feeding the ducks that were gathered at his feet. It reminded me of the many times that I fed the ducks at the retirement home, while visiting Grandma.

The weather was perfect. Perfect for spending a couple of hours, just relaxing. God knows I needed it, after the last few days I had had. The sun was shining; the birds were chirping. It wasn't too hot or too cool. It really was an idyllic day. It was especially nice to just sit and relax and let my worries be melted away by the warmth of the sun.

"Jack is that you? I haven't seen you in a while. How ya bin man?" A scruffy looking fellow asked, from the path behind me.

I almost gave myself away and answered when he called my name. It was hard to remember that I wasn't the person that people knew here, nor did I want to be. I continued to look straight ahead, in hopes that the man would think he was mistaken and move on.

"Jack is that you? Yeah it is. Still have the long hair? I would have thought you'd out - grown that by now," he said, from beside me now.

He looked like he was homeless. He wore many layers of clothes, even though it was a nice warm day. His hair was long and unkempt and there were leaves in it. His clothes were all frayed at the edges and he smelled faintly of urine and body odour. When he spoke, the teeth that remained were various colours of yellow, brown and even black. I had to turn my head for fear of gagging. The sight of his teeth coupled with the smell of his breath was overwhelming.

"I'm sorry Sir, but I can assure you, I have never met you before in my life," I said, in the most assuring voice I could manage.

"What's up with you? You in a witness protection program or something? I know it's you. A man doesn't forget someone he spent 2 years in a six by six cell with. Don't worry, I'm not going to blow your cover man. You know me. I wouldn't sing no matter how much they tortured me," he said, laughing loudly and clapping me on the shoulder.

The young boy and his Mother, that were feeding ducks, looked up uneasily at the sound of his laughter.

"Come on James, let's go," she said, grabbing his hand and leading him quickly down the path.

She checked over her shoulder several times as she walked along the path away from us. No doubt, checking to make sure we weren't following her.

"I'm sorry but you really do have me confused with someone else. I must be going. Have a nice day," I said, as I got up to leave.

"Sit the fuck down asshole! You're not going anywhere, until I say we're finished here. I spent the last year in that fuckin' cell, waiting for the day that I would see you again. I want my fuckin' money and I want it right fuckin' now. Understand?" he whispered in my ear, while forcing me back to a seated position.

At this point I realized that there was no point in arguing with him. He knew who I was, or who he thought I was, and he wasn't just going to let me go about my merry way.

"Let's go somewhere quieter, so we can catch up," he said, standing up beside me.

He had me at a complete disadvantage. I had no idea what he was talking about, and I figured at this point, the smart thing was to play along. That is if I didn't want to get myself beaten or worse, killed. Just keeping him at arm's length at this point would be a blessing. His breath was the vilest thing I had ever smelled in my life.

He led me down the street, around the corner and into a secluded back alley. I could feel the end of something hard jabbed against my ribs. I wasn't sure if it was a knife or a gun, but it didn't matter much. I was certain that he would have no problem killing me with either one and leaving me unceremoniously in this back alley. When we got to the end of the alley, he spun me around to face him. I assessed my chances of fighting back and decided against it. He was a giant of a man. Even though he was dishevelled and wore a lot of clothes, I could still see that he was in good shape physically. He was roughly the same height as me, but his shoulders were as wide as any linebacker's.

"What do ya say we catch up on old times?" he said mockingly.

"What do you have in mind?" I asked.

I needed him to take the lead in the conversation, because I really had no idea what he wanted, and I had no idea how bad Jack had crossed him.

"I was thinking that you give me my money, or I'll leave you for dead in this alley. How's that sound?" he said, baring his teeth.

"That doesn't sound very good to me at all. How much do you want?" I asked.

"All of it! You've had a year to come up with it, more than a year, and guess what? The year's up asshole!"

"I'm not playing games with you, honestly. I just don't remember how much we settled on," I said, trying not to let the fear creep into my voice.

"Five grand is what we settled on. I know you remember that. Stop playing games or you're gonna be sorry."

"I'm not. I can get your money. Just give me a little while to get it."

"You have a week. We'll meet at the same place, same time. You had better show up with my money, all of it, or I'll find you. You better believe I'll find you!" he said, as he stepped up really close to my face.

He looked me straight in the eyes for several agonizing seconds, before he turned without saying another word, walked out of the alley, around the corner and was gone.

I held my breath as he stared me in the eyes. Now that he was gone, I let it out, then inhaled deeply several times to catch my breath and to calm myself. I started to shake slightly as the unused adrenaline dissipated in my system. I squatted down and back up. It usually helped to speed up the process.

I walked back out of the alley and back into the park. I picked a secluded spot out of the way, where no one would see me.

If bad Jack ran into that guy before I did, which I hoped was the case, I wouldn't have to worry about him anymore. The thought made me feel a little guilty; just a little. Then the image of his mug shot, with the twisted grin came to mind and I no longer felt guilty. Karma, I thought. He deserved to have bad things happen to him; after all the pain that he had caused others.

It was time to put those thoughts behind me and just enjoy the beautiful day; something I had been trying to do, before Stinky ruined it. I sat with my eyes closed, letting the sun warm me and melt away my worries. The crimson-red glow of the sun through my eyelids was too bright. I slouched back in my seat and shielded my eyes with my arm. The darkness was comforting to my eyes and before I knew it, I was fast asleep.

I awoke with a start, disoriented and stiff. It took a few seconds to get my bearings and to figure out where I was. I rubbed at my sore neck with my left hand. My right arm had fallen asleep and was still all pins and needles. The sun had slipped to just above the tree tops. I glanced at my watch and saw that it was almost seven. I had been sleeping for hours. I felt refreshed, now that I was fully awake. I had however missed my window of opportunity to spy on bad Jack's Dad. At this point, I wasn't even sure that I still wanted to, or that I cared enough to bother. I would probably see it through, but tomorrow. I was hungry, and I just wanted to get home.

I got back to my place, made myself a pizza from the freezer and sat on the couch in front of the television to eat it. I avoided the news channels. I wanted to watch something carefree and the news was always bad. I settled on watching the comedy channel.

"Oh shit! I was going to touch base with the professor and I forgot" I said to the empty room.

Oh well. I would have to catch up with him tomorrow, when I went back.

The stand-up comedian on the T.V. made me laugh, despite my somewhat sombre mood, and I had forgotten about the troubling events of the day. When I went to bed that night, I was smiling and had a better outlook on life and what the next day might bring. Whoever said that laughter was the best medicine, might have been on to something.

CHAPTER NINE

The next morning, I went back to see if I could learn anything about bad Jack's Dad this time. I decided to leave my disguise as it was. His Mom didn't recognize me, so I figured that he probably wouldn't. The only reason that Stinky recognized me, was that he knew him when he had long hair. I could hardly imagine spending two years in a cell with that guy. It made my skin crawl, just thinking about it.

When I got there, I went straight to the office building where his Dad worked. I didn't really have a plan, not a good one anyway. I had no idea what I hoped to accomplish, but I had to keep moving forward, had to scratch that itch.

The down town core was greener than at home. The high rises looked taller and more modern, but they left room for lots of parks and parkettes everywhere. Where possible, they also had trees lining the middle of the roadway. Overall it had a very different feel about it. It was an urban setting, there was no denying that. It bustled and flowed at a faster pace than home, but it felt more in touch with nature all the same.

The street I was presently on, happened to be lined down the middle with a row of maples. There were breaks in the trees and the small curbs that contained them. These breaks were consistently placed mid-way down each block and they served as places to turn around. The sidewalks themselves were wider than I was accustomed to, no doubt to accommodate the heavier volume of pedestrian traffic. They weren't made of concrete either. They were made of interlocking stones. They were perfectly even and followed a pattern that repeated itself, the entire length of the sidewalk. Not a stone was out of place, not one was lifted or sunken. I marvelled at the consistency and wondered how they had accomplished it.

All the buildings on this block were well over thirty stories, with some topping fifty. The largest of them being the building where bad Jack's Dad worked. It was a large, shiny, black building with dark tinted glass and it was seventy-five stories tall. There was an awning that stretched ten feet on either side of the entrance and out to the curb at the front. There were men stationed at either side of the large double doors. They wore matching purple suits with gold trim and on their hands, they wore white gloves. It seemed that their sole purpose was to open the doors for visitors to the building. A steady stream of black limos dropped patrons off or picked them up. They were all very well-dressed individuals and I felt out of place. There was no doubt, that this office building catered to the richest of the rich.

It was such a contrast to see, compared to where his Mom worked. I wondered if his Dad knew what his wife did on the side, for extra spending money. It didn't look as if they were hurting for money, so maybe it wasn't for the money after all.

I approached the door man to my left. He greeted me cordially and opened the door for me. I was surprised to see that there were no security checks or police presence in the area at all. At home, there would have been both.

I entered the main foyer and looked around and then up. The sheer size of it, was nothing short of spectacular. In the middle of the room was a grand staircase that spiraled from a central point then split into two. One went to the left and one to the right and they joined again in the centre of the room on the third floor. It seemed as if the entire space was made of marble and polished brass or possibly even gold. One large chandelier hung from the centre of the room and extended from the ceiling on the third floor to above the second floor. It was made of crystal and the mixture of sunlight and artificial light was reflected in all directions. The result was tiny prisms of rainbow coloured light, dancing on the walls. The room was bustling with people. Men dressed in suits and women dressed in formal gowns. They looked like they were dressed for a dinner party, more than they looked like they were at work. The vastness of the area added to that perception. It reminded me of the foyer at a large Broadway theatre.

There were elevators at the back of the room, between the staircases. To the right of the entrance was a large counter with four young ladies stationed behind it. They wore purple dresses with gold trim, to match the doormen out front. A sign on the desk identified it as concierge. I approached the counter which was also marble with polished brass trim. One of the ladies looked up and smiled brightly at me.

"Can I help you Sir?" she asked, pleasantly.

"I hope so," I said, pausing to think for a split-second. I just realized that I had forgotten bad Jack's Dad's name. I decided to forge ahead, in hopes that she could fill in the blanks for me.

"Sorry, I've drawn a blank. I'm looking for a man, Armstrong is his last name. He is the C.E.O of a sporting goods retail chain and he has an office in this building. I'm sorry but I can't for the life of me, remember his first name," I said, rather embarrassed.

"Do you have an appointment?" she asked.

"No, I don't. I didn't realize I needed one," I said.

"It's fine, an appointment is not necessary. If he's not busy, he will still see you. He just likes to be prepared ahead of time for visitors. Who may I say is requesting a meeting with him?" she asked.

I hadn't expected this. I should have, I know, but I just wanted to know what floor he was on, so I could do a little recognisance. I didn't actually want to have a meeting with him. I struggled to come up with a plausible explanation, but for some reason my mind was a blank today and I failed miserably. I stood there blinking at her for some time, without replying. I thought for a moment that she may call security, but to my relief she didn't. Instead she did something completely unexpected.

"I'm due for a break. How'd you like to join me outside for a smoke?"

"Sure. Yeah. Okay," I stammered.

I wasn't sure what to expect, but I followed her outside and away from the entrance of the building. When we were far enough away, that her smoke wouldn't bother the waves of people entering and exiting the building; she stopped and lit her smoke.

"You don't smoke?" she asked, holding up her pack of cigarettes.

"No, I don't, thanks."

It wasn't until that second, that I recognized her for who she was. She looked vaguely familiar, but I couldn't place her. I thought at first, that she just had one of those faces that was familiar, but now it came to me. She obviously recognized me as well and that's why we were now standing on the sidewalk, while she enjoyed her smoke.

"So, what's your deal? You a private investigator or what?" she asked, casually.

She didn't seem at all upset or bothered by the idea that I might be.

"No, I'm not. I'm a teacher," I said.

"Okay, so why is a teacher spying on Mr. Armstrong? You'll have to forgive me, I haven't been with the firm all that long. Should I know you? I saw you yesterday morning, across the road from his house. It took me a while to place you, but now I know it's you. So, what's your deal? And be honest. I'll see through your bullshit," she said, matter of factly, taking a long haul on her cigarette and awaiting a response.

I didn't know what to say. The truth was not an option. She would think I was lying anyway.

"Let me help you out. You look like a good guy. You don't have to worry about me telling Armstrong anything that we talk about. I don't get caught up in the money and all the bullshit that goes with it. It's true what they say. Money can't buy happiness. Ain't that the truth, can I get an Amen," she rambled.

She sounded like a girl that needed to get a few things off her chest and I just happened to be the person she decided to talk to. I did find it odd that she called him Mr. Armstrong and not by his first name, but I was too busy trying to come up with a reasonable story, that I didn't give it much thought. Evidently, she had a lot on her mind as well, because she forgot to follow up on her question.

"I don't have long for break. Here's my card, give me a call sometime and we can meet for a drink and talk if you want."

"I'd like that," I said, and I meant it too.

I liked her. She had an engaging personality and I felt very comfortable with her.

"Okay, it's a date then," she said, uneasily.

"I'm Victoria, by the way," she said, holding out her hand.

"I'm Jack," I said, shaking her hand.

"Pleased to meet you, Jack," she said, smiling.

"Likewise, Victoria. It's been a pleasure."

"Come on, I'll point you in the right direction."

She could obviously tell from my blank stare, that I had no idea what she was referring to, and she filled in the blanks before I had to ask.

"Armstrong?" she said.

"Oh yeah, Armstrong," I said sheepishly.

I was too busy thinking about her name and then that got me thinking about my Victoria. I completely forgot about my spy mission. It now felt kind of stupid and insignificant.

"Come on space cadet," she said, laughing.

She meant no harm, but her words cut like a knife. I hoped that I didn't show just how much her words had affected me. I managed a small smile and walked to the door and held it open for her as she walked through.

I stood there for a minute trying to stay in the present, but old wounds surfaced, and I was back with Billy and Henry Johnson again.

I was eleven. Billy and Henry had left me alone for the better part of a year. After the incident with my hat, they didn't bother me for a while when they realized that their bullying didn't affect me. Like I said before, the wisdom that Grandma had given me on that fateful day stuck with me for a bit but was soon forgotten. Billy and Henry spent their time picking on other kids, but eventually they made their way back to me. They were delighted to find, that when they picked on me this time, it made me miserable. Actually, Billy was the one that seemed to enjoy it. Henry seemed as though he was just following along. I always seemed to be thinking of too many things at once. Today, they might say that I suffered from attention deficit disorder, but that wasn't it. I just had a vivid imagination and I enjoyed being able to escape my life at times and imagine other things. That fit nicely as it turned out, with my ability to travel.

Billy, more so then Henry, loved to torment me. He would call me names and slap me and trip me whenever he felt like it. I responded by not responding. I just picked myself and continued, but there was no hiding the fact, that his antics bothered me greatly. On several occasions, to the delight of Billy, I was brought to tears, but I just kept walking, in hopes that he would lose interest and move on to picking on someone else. For whatever Billy was, he was certainly no quitter. Once he started, he intended on seeing it through, until he was satisfied that he had made my life as miserable as possible.

His favourite name for me was of course, space cadet. Why he chose this particular name, I can't be sure. I think it may have stemmed from my seemingly distant and vacant stare that I adopted whenever he picked on me. I just kind of zoned out and kept moving, hoping that he would stop. It was a way of me trying to protect myself from all the hurtful things that he did and said. For the most part, it worked, but still some of it got through. I couldn't block all his negative energy.

Henry followed along with his brother's actions, but even as a kid, I understood that he was just trying to survive, the same as me. He didn't show the same vigor and determination as his big brother. His heart wasn't in it.

Billy, on the other hand, relished his role as bully and endeavoured to be the best he could be at his craft. He never missed an opportunity to kick someone when they were down or to point out someone's weaknesses or deficiencies.

He would stand in my way as I tried to walk past him. When I refused to answer him, he yelled at me, and got madder still. This would usually lead to him calling me a space cadet, while yelling, from within an inch of my face.

"Can you hear me, space cadet?" he yelled, drops of spit spraying across my face.

Even then, I found it to be a little amusing. The sheer ridiculousness of the situation was surreal. Billy asking if I could hear him, while he yelled at the top of his lungs, from an inch in front of my face. I kept that to myself, however. Laughing now, would almost certainly land me in the hospital, so I looked at my feet and he continued to yell. On these types of occasions, Henry sometimes tried to intervene, but Billy put him in his place quickly and he backed off. He would be off to the side, looking down and shuffling his feet back and forth.

"Are you fuckin' deaf or just stupid, or maybe both?" he asked.

I didn't answer. It sounded like a rhetorical question to me. He couldn't possibly expect an answer to such a moronic line of questioning. Ah, but he did. He flew into a rage when I ignored him, or more accurately, tuned him out.

"I'm talking to you space cadet, and you'd better fuckin' answer me or I swear I'm goin' to fuck you up real bad!" he continued to yell.

I had no reason to believe that he wasn't telling the truth and so I mumbled some sort of answer. It seemed to satisfy him for the moment. He really wasn't interested in what I had to say anyway. He usually worked himself into a bit of a frenzy and once he had begun, there was no stopping him until he had had enough. Henry had learned by this point not to interfere when he got this way. He just kept his head down and waited for Billy to finish.

Finally, he'd had enough of me and he punched me hard in the mouth and nose with his right fist. Bright stars exploded in front of my eyes. I went reeling backwards and would have surely smashed my head on the curb behind me, if it weren't for Henry catching me. Blood spilled from both nostrils and a large split in my upper lip. I spit a large mass of blood and saliva onto the sidewalk beside me and then looked back through tear blurred eyes to where Billy had been standing. He was no longer there. He had moved to beside me and Henry. Henry let me fall to the ground as gently as he could and then turned to face his older brother. His face was twisted with rage. His face was blood red and he was panting wildly. He charged forward, like a bull charging a matador. He meant to tackle him to the ground and lay a beating on him I'm sure, but he never got the chance. Billy was still charging forward with his arms outstretched in front of him reaching for his waist. Henry pistoned his left leg up hard and caught him flush in the face. I'm not sure if it was just a reaction or if he'd finally had enough of Billy's bullying over the years, but the result was the same regardless. Billy's broken nose sprayed blood all over his face, on Henry's jeans and a few droplets even found their way to the left shoulder of the t-shirt I was wearing. He collapsed in a heap, unconscious. Henry had a shocked look on his face when he turned toward me. I must have had the same look on my face as well. He turned back toward his brother and knelt beside him. He put his ear to Billy's face and listened to him breathe.

"He's alright, just unconscious. Boy, is he gonna be pissed when he comes to. You had better not be here when he does. I'll stay to make sure he's okay, you'd better bugger off."

"I think you're right. Thanks Henry."

"Don't mention it. He had it coming to him," he said, and then turned to face Billy again.

That was the last time I ever saw him alive.

His death was officially listed as an accident. Billy and Henry were at the quarry out on Colver lane, some time after he had broken Billy's nose. He wasn't too happy with him after that incident, but he seemed to have come to terms with it. He didn't react violently as I had expected he would, but he became sullen and withdrawn instead. He even left me alone afterward; which came as a complete surprise to me.

Apparently, on that fateful day, Billy and Henry were going to go down the steep cliff and go swimming, but before they could, Henry lost his footing and fell the more than sixty feet to the gravel floor below, missing the water as he did.

There was a police investigation of course, but they concluded that there was no foul play.

I wasn't sure myself at the time. I knew Billy was an asshole, but I had a hard time believing that he would murder his own brother. They were inseparable for as long as I could remember, and I just couldn't believe that even he, was capable of such a thing.

There have been facts that have come out since that shocked me, and the entire community for that matter. Facts about what kind of monster Billy Johnson really was. A local author wrote a biography of sorts about him called The Suffering and it shed a light on his troubled life.

My terrible trip down memory lane now concluded, I followed Victoria back into the foyer of the office building. She took up her position behind the counter and then pointed me in the right direction.

"So, we're getting together later?" she asked.

"I'm not sure what my plans are, but I'll call I promise," I said and turned to walk in the direction of the elevators.

"Okay, talk to you later then."

The elevators were all set in a long row at the back of the room, between the staircases. There were eight in total. There was a non-stop parade of people entering and exiting, and all of them seemed to be in a hurry. All except for me. I must have stuck out like a sore thumb. I was having reservations about continuing with my somewhat dubious plan of spying on bad Jack's Dad. What was I going to do if I came face to face with him? But, then again, he was likely in his office or a board room and I would never see him anyway. I paused at the entrance to the elevator for a moment, deciding whether to continue on or go back. The people behind me made the decision for me. I was swept into the elevator by a wave of humanity, pushing me along and into the elevator.

It reminded me of the countless Doctor Who books I had read as a kid. The elevator seemed impossibly large on the inside, much the same as the Doctor's phone booth. The elevator was lined with mirrors and a brass hand rail that ran around its perimeter at waist height. It was the strangest elevator ride I had ever been on in my life. There was a loud murmur of voices coming from the many different conversations that continued throughout the ride to the 72nd floor. I was used to elevator rides with everyone staring straight ahead or at their feet, in perfect silence.

The ride itself took a very short time. It was without a doubt the fastest elevator I had ever been on in my life. When the elevator came to a stop, my stomach flip flopped from the sudden change and a strange sense of vertigo overcame me. I reached for the hand rail to steady myself. The feeling passed quickly, but I found myself alone in the elevator. All the other riders were no doubt used to the speed of the elevator and they were out and on their way. I followed soon behind them, but not before I got dirty looks from several people that were waiting to enter the elevator to make the return trip down to terra firma.

I walked past the unhappy, would-be elevator riders and stopped in the hallway, away from the front of the elevators. There was a water fountain part way up the hall and I made my way toward it. The cool water was refreshing and did wonders to help the uneasy feeling in my belly go away. That was short lived however.

Two men were coming down the hallway toward me. There was no place to hide. I buried my face in the fountain again, hoping that they would continue past me and down the hall. No such luck. They stopped behind me and waited their turn. The man directly behind me was waiting to get a drink from the fountain. The other man, who just happened to be bad Jack's Father, took up position just fifteen feet away. My heart was pounding, and

I didn't know what to do. I kept my head down for the moment and kept drinking. I couldn't stay that way for ever, so I finally stood up. I pretended to dribble some water on my chin and covered my mouth with my hand as I turned and walked in the direction that the two men had just come from.

"Hey buddy, you dropped something," Bad Jack's Dad called after me.

I ignored him and kept walking. He called out again, and again I ignored him and kept walking. My heart was now pounding like a jack hammer in my chest. My mouth went dry, despite the copious amount of water I had just consumed. I started to sweat, and by the time I made the corner and was out of sight, dark rings of sweat appeared under my armpits. I was afraid that he might follow me, so I ducked into the first door that I came to.

My face was covered with sweat and I felt a little light headed. I looked up to find a waiting room full of people staring at me. I sat in in the closest chair and tried to re-group. The people went back to talking and reading their magazines, and about their business as before.

I noticed a newspaper sitting on the small table beside me. On the front cover was none other than bad Jack's Father. His Father had a name after all. It was Karl. I couldn't remember his name for the life of me, but yeah Karl, that was it, now I remembered.

The headline read: Prominent businessman denounces son after dismissal of charges. There was a picture of Karl surrounded by reporters in front of this very building and another picture of bad Jack with a rip between the two of them. The caption below the picture said: A family torn apart. The picture of bad Jack was the same creepy mug shot that I had seen before. I set the paper back on the table, not wanting to read it. I was surprised to see that the paper was still here after all this time. Perhaps people were just fascinated by the fact that he worked in this very building and so the story took on a life of its own. I for one had read the story already and I had no desire to read it again. It was disturbing to say the least.

I decided that it was probably safe to leave now. I had calmed down. I had stopped sweating and my heart rate had returned to normal. I made my way out into the hall and to the elevators and left the building without incident.

I went straight home from there. I had had enough for one day. When I got home I flopped on the couch and relaxed for a bit. My thoughts drifted toward my Vicki and the Vicki that I had met earlier. I reached into my back pocket to retrieve the card that she had given me. It wasn't in my pocket, so I checked the other pocket. It wasn't there either. I reached into each of my two front pockets but neither one produced the card that I was looking for.

That's when it hit me. I dropped it in the hallway after I saw Karl Armstrong. That's why he was yelling after me. I dismissed it as unimportant. I'm sure that I wasn't the first person that she had given a card to, that never called her. I did promise to call her however, and for that I did feel a little guilty, but I had a lot on my mind and so my thoughts drifted elsewhere.

CHAPTER TEN

The next morning, I struggled to not phone Vicki, but ultimately, I respected her wishes and resisted calling. I had no intentions of continuing with my foolish quest to see my birth parents. I was extremely glad that my Grandma had done me the favour of switching me at birth. The next order of business was to re-connect with the professor. I didn't want him to think that I was blowing him off. He might very well prove to be someone that I may need in the future and I needed to keep him in the loop. Besides, I found that although we had only just met, I liked him very much. I ate breakfast and began getting ready to go see the professor. There was a knock on my door.

"Just a minute, I'm just getting dressed," I said, hoping that it might be Vicki at the door.

There was no answer. I hurriedly got dressed and went to the door. I looked through the peep hole and was pleased to see the professor standing there, patiently waiting for the door to open.

"Hello my boy! Hope I'm not intruding. When I was last here you seemed to be out of sorts, not surprising under the circumstances. I hope we can cheer you up," he said, smiling an impossibly wide smile.

I was confused for a second, until his identical twin stepped out from behind the door. He was followed by another and then another. I laughed with delight. It was such a surreal experience to see four of them all standing in a row on my front step. I stood staring at them; looking from one to the next, up and down the line.

"Can we come in?" the professor asked.

"Of course, come in! Where are my manners? Come in! Come in!" I said, beckoning them forward, into the house.

They wasted no time coming in, removing their shoes and awaiting further instruction.

"Come, let's sit in the living room. Make yourself comfortable. Can I get you anything?" I asked enthusiastically.

"Do you have any beer?" the professor asked.

"I do. I replenished my stock after my binge the other night. It is morning though, are you sure?" I asked.

"Absolutely! We're in the mood to let loose, and I think you could loosen up a little bit yourself. I'll replace what we drink later, that's not a problem," he said, clapping his hands together, removing his coat and rolling up his sleeves.

His counter-parts did the same and sat patiently waiting.

I went into the kitchen and put some new beers into the refrigerator, removed five and took them into the living room. I placed them on the coffee table, grabbed mine, opened it and took a swig.

"Let me introduce you to my brother and my brothers from another Mother. This handsome devil is my brother Dale," he said, nudging the man to his left.

Dale stood up, stepped forward and shook my hand.

"Pleased to meet you."

This was repeated by the other two men, whom as it turns out were named Doug and Hank.

"I filled my brothers in, about you being able to move between the worlds, as we can. I hope that wasn't too presumptuous of me?" the professor said.

"No, not at all. If anyone would understand, it would be the four of you."

"Quite right! Very good, I would say. Now let's have some fun, shall we?" he said, tipped up his bottle of beer, and finished it in one swallow.

Dale, Doug and Hank followed suit. It seemed to me, that the professor was the unofficial leader of the bunch. The other three tended to watch to see what he did before they followed. They did however loosen up after a few beers and their respective personalities began to shine through. All of them were outgoing and fun to be around. They certainly knew how to have a good time and I was swept up in their jovial lust for life and all my troubles were forgotten. They all had great infectious laughs and the comical stories flowed like the beer. Hank was the biggest prankster of the bunch and Dale turned out to be the comic. The professor and Doug seemed to fit nicely somewhere in between. Sometime during the day and into the night, the professor implored me to call him Bruce instead of professor, and so he was from that day forward, known as Bruce.

I had bought two cases of beer the day before, and they were gone when supper rolled around. We decided to go out for supper and on the way back they insisted on stopping at the store to replace the beer that they had drunk. That was short lived, because before the night was through, one of the cases had been polished off. They sure could drink for little fellas.

I thought about asking them if they were from Irish descent, based upon their ability to drink, but I wasn't sure if that would be an insult. I imagined that they would take it as a compliment anyway. Then again, I wasn't positive that there was even an Ireland in the other world. I realized just how much I didn't know about that world.

"Doing some thinking there again, I see. My brothers and I are going to have to work on you a bit, I would say. You need to learn to let go. Have some fun!" Bruce said.

"Maybe I can help. Let me see...there must be a joke or two rattling around in there. Okay...yes, here we go. Did you know I was married?" Dale asked.

"Well I am and she's a nice lady, but I haven't talked to her in three days. I didn't want to interrupt her."

Dale slapped his knee and laughed and laughed, beer spraying out his nose, which just made everyone laugh that much more. He set his beer on the table and rubbed his hands together in front of his face, clearly trying to come up with another joke.

"Never mind. I can't seem to think of one."

"Usually we can't get him to stop telling jokes," Bruce said.

"So, you are married?" I asked.

"Yeah, you know what? When we first got married we bought a little house out in the country. We didn't have a lot of money, but I had to have a big screen television. I love T.V. you know? Anyway, I bought one of those remotes. What do you call them? They do it all."

"A universal remote?" I asked.

"Yeah, that's it. And you know what? That changed everything," he said and broke into another fit of laughter, followed by the other three.

"Very funny," I said, joining them in laughter, although it had more to do with their reactions than the joke itself.

"So, you're not married then?" I asked.

"Oh God no. Why would I want to go and do a fool thing like that?" Dale said.

Dale told a few more jokes and Hank pulled a few pranks. They were both very adept at mis-directing your attention, to get maximum effect for their efforts. The other two kept it light, telling stories about all the trouble that they had gotten themselves into over the years.

When the night of merriment had concluded, I tried to make them as comfortable as possible. Bruce and Dale slept in the spare room and Doug and Hank slept on the couch and love seat respectively. We didn't hit the hay until around 3 A.M., so they weren't too worried about comfort and they seemed just fine with their sleeping arrangements.

It was a long day as it turned out. The muscles in my face hurt from so much laughing. I couldn't remember having more fun in one day. These guys were a blast to have around, something that has continued over the years since.

I went to sleep with a smile on my face that night. It was the first in a very long time for me. I was thankful that Grandma had introduced me to the professor, or Bruce. Old habits die hard I guess. It would take a while, but eventually I would come to think of him as Bruce and not the professor.

The next morning the four brothers were funny but in a different way. All of them had hangovers, and I'm not certain that they weren't still a little drunk from the previous night's escapades. I was up at 9 A.M. and they got up around 10. Dale begged me to draw the shades in the living room, and I obliged with a bit of a laugh.

"What's the matter boys, getting a little old to drink like that anymore?" I teased.

Not an answer from any of them. They sat at the kitchen table with their heads in their hands. Not a word was spoken for quite some time. Occasionally, a groan or a fart escaped one of them and broke the silence. Once in a while, one of their heads would slip from their hands and go plummeting towards the table and get jerked back up violently, just before making contact with the table's surface. Slowly but surely, they started to come around. It took an hour or so, but then they were poking fun at each other and laughing again. I could only hope to have their zest for life at their age, Hell, what was I thinking, I didn't have their energy now.

"I had a great time last night, thank you," I said.

"We did too." Bruce said, but they all agreed. "It's been a while since we all got together to let off some steam. I for one am starting to feel my age, I would say." They all murmured in agreement to that statement as well.

"What do you say we all go out and get a bite to eat? After I recover a bit more that is," Dale said.

"Sounds good to us," they all agreed.

"Yeah after a little more recovery time," Bruce added.

"Sounds good to me as well," I said.

First things first though. I had to brush my teeth before I went any farther. I came out of the bathroom, refreshed from the now clean taste in my mouth. I had splashed some cold water on my face as well, and I was ready to start the day.

The guys were wide awake now and in full slapstick mode. They were constantly teasing and poking each other. It was all done in fun and they all seemed to enjoy it. They reminded me of a bunch of teenagers and they were great fun to be around. I still couldn't believe that they were as old as they were. They were older than my parents and I would never see my parents act as they did, that was for sure.

We went to a restaurant close by for brunch. Not only could these guys drink for little guys, but they sure could eat as well. The effects of drinking too much alcohol seemed to be behind them now and they were livelier than ever. The waitress was amazed to see the four identical men and engaged in lively conversation with them throughout our meal. In fact, everyone in the restaurant took their turn staring at them. It's not every day, that you see identical quadruplets, especially with the larger than life personalities of those four.

During the day we spent together, we did find some time to discuss matters related to twins and travelling. They had a lot of experience with travelling, and twins of course, but their personal experiences were of no help to me. They were not opposites like other twins. They were all friendly and their families were aware of one another and actually visited on a regular basis. Their situation really was quite different than my mine. I enjoyed hearing their stories nevertheless and had a great time in their company, but Grandma had covered all the bases.

"I wish we could have been more help to you, but alas, your situation is much different than our own, I would say," Bruce said.

"Yeah, what he said. If you ever need our help; we're at your disposal," Hank said.

"You never know when you'll need a hand, but if you ever do, just ask," Dale said.

"Ditto," Doug said.

"That's it, ditto. That's all you have to add?" Bruce teased.

Doug laughed. "I had nothing to say. I didn't want to be left out."

Dale, Doug and Hank left after much ado about how much fun they had and how much they enjoyed meeting me. I assured them that I enjoyed meeting them as well and that we would surely be seeing each other again. They seemed genuinely excited about the prospect of getting together again.

Bruce stayed behind after the other three had gone.

"So, what do you think? I told you they were real characters, didn't I?"

"As advertised. I enjoyed that, and I really needed that, thank you."

"Don't mention it. You struck me as a fellow that could use a little cheering up. I don't want to be a downer, but we have to figure out what we are going to do about this bad Jack of yours," he said, his normal jovial appearance replaced with a concerned look on his face.

"First things first. Why don't you tell me what's got you all in a tither where he's concerned? I know your Grandma warned you about him, warned you again and again, as a matter of fact. I know that he has recently started to travel. Has he made contact with you?"

So, there it was. The question that begged to be answered. The one that I had been avoiding. The answer to that question, was what had changed my life into this tumultuous existence for the past few weeks.

The short answer was, no. No, bad Jack had not contacted me, nor had he tried to. It was far worse than that. He had contacted Vicki.

"No, he hasn't contacted me, but he did pose as me to get close to Vicki. This was concerning of course but now that I know more about him, it's even more disconcerting. I don't even know what to think or what I'm doing half the time. I have to stop worrying about me. I should be protecting her."

"Wow, I see what you mean. Given his track record, I think we need to have someone watch out for her, when you can't. Hank has a friend that would be perfect for the job. I'm sure he'll be up for it. I'll see if he can get on it straight away. Can't you tell Vicki about him and to be careful, to watch herself?"

"I would but she didn't believe me when I tried to tell her that it wasn't me that was acting strangely, but him. She thought I was lying or off my rocker, or both. She has made it very clear that she wants some space, but I think that is a wonderful idea, to have someone watch over her. It would really set my mind at ease."

"I'm confident that Hank's friend will do it and if he's tied up with something else, I'm positive he'll know someone that can help us. Don't worry, I have it covered," he reassured me.

I believed in him and I felt much better, knowing that Vicki would be looked after.

Bad Jack must have been doing some reconnaissance of his own. I'm not entirely sure how much he knows about me and I'm almost certain that I must know more about him, than he does about me. He isn't necessarily playing by the same rules as I am though. Grandma did a good job of explaining to me all about travelling and gave me a lot of useful information.

I'm not sure where he got his info from.

"I'm going to watch over her from a distance as well, as best as I can anyway," I said.

"That sounds good, very good, I would say. Well, in the meantime, when I can, I'm going to find out as much as I can about this bad Jack character. I know a lot of people, and I would like to think that I'm well enough connected that I might have some pull back home. I know everything will work out just fine. You'll see."

He sounded very confident and it did a lot to set my mind at ease.

"Thanks for all your help, I really appreciate it."

"No problem at all my boy; glad to do it. I do think it's time that I get going though. I'll keep in touch and I'll let you know when Hank's friend is on Vicki's tail and if he sees anything," he said, then got up.

Shortly thereafter he was gone, and I was alone again.

Back to bad Jack... His hair was cut the same as mine. Stinky obviously knew him when he had long hair, but it wasn't now. His outward appearance was remarkably similar to mine. Sometimes when I saw a picture of him, it would take me a second to be able to tell if it was him or me.

I'm not sure if he set out to find Vicki or if he just bumped into her, but he knew who she was nevertheless. Actually, I'm not even entirely sure about that either. He may just have played along with her until he figured it out. I don't know what happened during that first encounter. She just acted funny when she got home and didn't say anything. It wasn't until later, that I found out that something had happened.

She was upset about two weeks after that first incident and she was yelling at me and began recalling some of the strange things that I had said or did. I of course didn't have a clue what she was talking about. That made her angrier still. She said that I never remembered anything that we talked about, because I never made her a priority and it escalated from there. She wanted to know what was going on with me. She said that I wasn't acting like myself, that I had been acting strangely. She even asked me if I was having an affair, because of something that I had said. It was a no-win situation for me. It took me quite some time before I realized that she had been talking to bad Jack and not to me. That is a big part of the reason that I never told her about him. She had already decided that she wanted a break, before I realized what had been happening.

If I had just been up front with her and told her or showed her like I showed Helen, then all of this could have been avoided. I made a mess of this and I was going to fix it. I just hoped that Vicki would understand why I didn't tell her. I know that is asking a lot of her, but I believe that she will come around. Once she lets me back in to her life, I'm confident that we can do whatever is necessary to live a long and happy life together.

CHAPTER ELEVEN

I remember it like it was yesterday. It was a beautiful early fall afternoon. You know, the kind of day that you couldn't possibly improve upon, if you tried. There were wisps of clouds here and there, in an otherwise perfectly blue sky. The humidity from summer had now left us and the air was warm, but felt lighter, cleaner. The leaves hadn't started to turn yet, and the birds were singing loudly in the trees. The lawn was full of students loafing around, lying on the grass or sitting on the many benches. They were enjoying the weather the same as I was. I always liked the fall more than any other season. It's not too cold and not too warm, with no humidity. Fall is special. It is the last chance to enjoy the outdoors, before the cold of winter comes.

It was my second year of college. I was completely caught up on all my studies except for some mandatory reading that I had to complete before the month was out. It was as good a time as any, to do it that day. I sat up against a tree, with my book in hand, basking in the warmness of the sun's rays. Occasionally, I would stop to take in the day and enjoy all that was around me, then dive back in between the pages of my book. When I read, I am so fully immersed in that world, that my mind completely shuts off from the real world. I remember everything about that day, but now that I think of it, I have no idea what book I was reading. I guess that's because it wasn't important to my story. Once in a while, a friend of mine would make a point of stopping and saying hi and pulling me out of the pages of the book and back into our world. It took me several minutes to burrow back beneath the pages and immerse myself again. I was not quite fully back in, and so I noticed when someone leaned up against the tree to my right. I continued to read all the same and didn't really pay much attention.

"What a beautiful afternoon. Don't you think?" she asked.

I was never much good at small talk. I was of course, a bit of an introvert; not surprising given my childhood. I wouldn't say I was shy. That would imply that I got nervous around people. That wasn't the case at all. I just didn't care to get close to people, because other than my immediate family, no one else had ever treated me particularly well.

I answered her because I didn't want to be rude, but I truly just wanted to be left alone.

"Yeah, it sure is," I said, without looking up, trying to keep it short.

"Hi, I'm Vicki," she said happily, thrusting her hand above my book for me to shake.

I grabbed her hand and shook it, then looked over at her. She had a great smile and she knew how to use it. Little dimples appeared at the sides of her mouth. Her teeth were showing, and they were the whitest teeth I had ever seen. She wasn't beautiful in the sense that she could be a model or anything. She was good looking for sure, but it was her smile that I remember most from that first encounter. She was beautiful, in a girl-next-door, comfortable way.

"Hi I'm Jack," I answered.

I meant to leave it at that, but she apparently had other ideas.

"Nice to meet you Jack. That's a solid name, a strong name. I like it."

At this point I closed my book and decided to give her my full attention and not be rude. We ended up talking for quite some time about anything and everything. She was easy to talk to, fun to talk to and I really enjoyed myself. Eventually however, I had to go and so I got up to leave.

"Well, it was nice meeting you Vicki. I have to go, but maybe I'll see you around campus," I said.

"That's it!" she said.

She sounded annoyed with me, but I wasn't sure what I had done.

"I'm sorry. I don't follow you. Did I offend you somehow?" I said, puzzled.

"Well that depends. Do you have a girlfriend?"

"No," I said, still confused.

I'm not always the quickest person to pick up on messages that others are sending me, especially when it comes to the opposite sex.

She ripped a page out of her book and quickly scribbled something on the piece of paper, folded it and then handed it to me. I went to grab it from her, but she held it in her hand for several seconds before letting it go.

"Yeah, I hope I'll see you around too, Jack," she said, winked at me, got up and walked away.

She turned and waved to me once, then disappeared into the crowd of students making their way back to class.

I waited until she was out of sight before I opened the piece of paper. To be honest, at the time, I never gave it much thought. I found her attractive, but I never thought that there would be anything more than me remembering the nice girl that I had talked to, that one day at school. That was of course, until I opened the folded piece of paper that she had given me, and read it.

She had scribbled the note so quickly that at first, I had difficulty making out the words. I skipped over the note, right to the bottom of the page where she had written her phone number. I smiled and returned to the top of the page to see what she had written.

It read:

I enjoyed meeting you and I hope you feel the same. Call me sometime. Soon! Vicki.

I continued to smile as I read what she had written. She had obviously picked up on the fact that I was a little unsure around women, based on the end of the conversation that we had had. I could tell from what she had written, that she knew that if I put it off, then I would find reasons to never call. I could also tell that she really hoped that I called. You're probably wondering how I got all that from what she had written. I guess I'm just very intuitive, that, and she also told me afterwards.

One of the many things that I always liked about her, was that she is more outgoing than me. I'm a little too reserved for even my liking sometimes. So, I went out of my comfort zone right then and there. I grabbed my cell phone from my back pocket and dialed the number at the bottom of the paper.

"Hello?" Vicki answered.

"Is this too soon?" I asked.

"Jack. Is that you?" she asked. I could tell from her voice that she was smiling.

"Well, you said soon. I figured I might lose my nerve, if I didn't call right away."

"I figured that as well. That's why I said soon! Okay, you have my undivided attention. What did you have in mind?"

"I'm not sure. I never really thought past calling you," I said, laughing uneasily.

"Well the traditional thing to do, would be for you to take me out for dinner and maybe a movie."

"Okay, I'm up for that. Where and when would you like to go?"

"I'm not a traditional girl. I'm walking back toward you right now. I have a good feeling about you Jack. You had better not turn out to be a creep," she said.

I wasn't sure how to respond. I looked up and saw her walking toward me. She waved at me and I heard the click of her phone, hanging up in my ear. I put my phone away and watched as she walked to me.

"Come on. Let's go, I'm taking you to my favourite place for lunch," she said, looping her arm through mine and pulling me with her.

We walked on the path for a while, before cutting across the grass and onto the sidewalk that ran the length of the large lawn in front of the campus. We talked, and she made me feel comfortable and at ease; something that felt alien to me, especially on a first date. She laughed easily, and she grabbed my arm or shoulder when she did. We walked for quite some time until we were in a part of town that I had been to before but wasn't too familiar with.

"Here it is!" she exclaimed, throwing her arms in the air.

The sign out front was sandwiched between two trees, with vines running down either side and snaking their way around and around as they did. They were covered in huge green leaves the size of footballs. The lush green of the leaves continued into the garden below. The garden itself surrounded a small pond that held fish, turtles and frogs. A large parrot sat on a perch, close to the door. It looked as though we were peering into the rainforest, in some remote, far - off location. Sounds of birds and monkeys drifted toward us from within.

The name of the restaurant was The Jungle, and I quickly came to understand why it was her favourite restaurant. The inside was much the same as the outside. Potted plants covered the walls, and trees were placed anywhere that there was space for them. Ivy and philodendrons slinked their way across the large wooden beams that served as roof trusses. Birds flew from tree to tree. Some were brightly coloured finches and others were parrots or parakeets. I even saw a couple pygmy marmosets briefly, as they climbed farther into the canopies of their respective trees and disappeared.

Vicki was delighted to watch my reaction, with every new discovery that I made. She was beaming every time I looked at her. This was all, before we were seated at our table.

The waiters and waitresses all wore khaki shirts and shorts, hiking boots and a brimmed hat.

"Welcome to The Jungle, my name is Clayton and I'll be your server this afternoon. Hey Vicki, nice to see you again. Is this your first time to The Jungle, Sir?" he asked.

"It sure is, but I can tell you, that it won't be the last," I said, not able to contain my excitement.

"Hi Clayton, good to see you too," she said.

Clayton took our drink orders. Our choices were limited to water or juices. Everything was natural and eco-friendly in The Jungle. I chose orange juice and she just had a water. The menu itself consisted of all manners of traditional items that were of course, all-natural as well. There were burgers and nachos, fish, beef and chicken items. All pretty normal restaurant fare. She convinced me to try the items at the back of the menu, however. She ordered, and we shared a plate. These items were about as far from normal as I could possibly imagine. To be quite honest, if it hadn't been our first date, I would have passed on her choice of table fare. She was from the first date, as it turned out, very good at getting me to do things out of my comfort zone. The sample plate that sat in front of me looked normal enough, and it smelled good as well. It wasn't until she told me what hid beneath, that my stomach did a bit of a flip. The first thing that I noticed was chicken feet and combs that were deep fried, golden brown. There were deep fried frog legs as well. There was a side order of sweet potato fries with chipotle mayo. Finally, something that I recognized. The next item looked normal enough as well, until I saw what was inside. It was a partially formed duckling, inside an egg. I watched as she enjoyed it, but I couldn't bring myself to try it. There was some alligator in some sort of delicious red sauce, loaded with onions and beans. In the middle of the plate, was a small dish with chicken liver pate in it. I tried it, but it wasn't something that I enjoyed. She looked like she was truly enjoying the food. I on the other hand, had mixed feelings. The alligator was delicious and the sweet potato fries were good. The chicken feet and combs weren't too bad, and either were the frog legs. She gave me full marks for at least trying them and keeping an open mind. It seemed like a bit of a test to me; to find out how open I could be to new ideas.

Lunch wasn't finished yet, not quite. Dessert was yet to come. It was chocolate ice cream covered with tiny sprinkles of chocolate, that just happened to be chocolate covered ants. It was actually quite tasty. The ants were chocolatey and a little crunchy. I was surprised that I enjoyed it and even ordered it every time that I ate there in the future.

We spent the rest of the afternoon together. We talked and laughed and got to know each other better. When we parted ways, I felt that I had truly met someone special, someone that I wanted to get to know better.

The next morning, I awoke with a smile on my face, thinking about the day that I had spent with Vicki. I couldn't wait to see her again, but I didn't want to seem like a creep and bug her right away. I waited a day before calling her, even though it seemed like a week.

The next day, my plan was to take her to my favourite restaurant and then go down by the river for a walk. When I called her, all I got was an answering machine.

"Hi Vicki. It's Jack. I wanted to say that I had a great time the other day and I hope that we can get together soon," I said, to her answering machine.

I hung up the phone, disappointed that I hadn't gotten to talk to her, hoping that she would call me back. A few seconds later, the phone rang, and I snatched it up, and answered it excitedly.

"Hello," I said, hopefully.

"Is this Jack Armstrong?"

"Yes, it is."

"Do you have a moment to answer a few questions about how satisfied you are with your cell phone service? It will only take a few seconds."

I hung up the phone without saying a word. The excited feeling being replaced with one of disappointment.

Minutes turned into hours and then into days and she still hadn't called back. I thought that maybe I misread that she had enjoyed my company as much as I had enjoyed hers. Perhaps, I thought, I didn't pass her little test after all.

A week had gone by and I started to think that maybe she hadn't gotten the message that I left on her answering machine, after all. I thought I would leave another message and if she didn't return my call, then try to forget about Vicki and move on with my life.

I left another message, trying to sound as nonchalant as possible, but I feared that I may have failed miserably. I nearly called back to try and repair some of the damage, but I decided against it. I was nearly certain that it would do more harm than good.

Nearly two weeks passed and still no word from her. I tried to move on, forget about her, but found that I was having a hard time doing that. It had taken just that one afternoon to hook me. She pulled me in with her wittiness and her spontaneity, kindness and intelligence. She wasn't bad to look at either; I can't forget that.

I tried to resume my normal life, and for the most part I succeeded. She had made a lasting impression to be sure, but we are all creatures of habit, and so I resumed my life without Vicki in it. Once in a while, I would think of her or even go visit The Jungle to get something to eat, in hopes that I might bump into her.

Five weeks went by and I had given up any hope of ever seeing her again.

I came home from class, put my books on the chair by the door and ran for the bathroom. I made it in time, but just. I was in a hurry; it had been a long day and I just wanted to get home and relax. I didn't want to stop to use the bathroom at the school and I guess I underestimated how badly I had to go.

When I emerged from the bathroom I flopped on my bed and turned on the television. The remote was acting up and I figured that it probably needed new batteries. I kept some spares in the telephone stand. When I got them out of the drawer, I noticed that the light on the answering machine was blinking. I hit the button and then flopped on my bed again.

There was a message from my friend Jamie, about a party on Friday night and then after a long pause, a girl's voice broke the silence of my room. It was a short message, and even though it had been weeks since I'd heard her voice, there was no doubt who it was.

"Hey Jack, call me," she said quietly.

I replayed the message, listening intently. I erased the message from Jamie and played the message from Vicki two more times. After all this time, and that's all she had to say. I didn't know what to make of it. I was a little pissed off, to be honest. She calls me, and I'm supposed to jump when she says so. Well, I wasn't going to jump just because she said so. I tried out the remote again, now that it had fresh batteries. It worked flawlessly. I turned up the volume and flicked through the channels trying to find something to watch. No matter how many times I changed the channel and no matter how many different things I chose to occupy my thoughts, only one thought prevailed. Vicki. She kept creeping into my thoughts and I couldn't shake her.

I wasn't going to jump, but I was going to call her. Who was I kidding? I was always going to call her. What happened after that, depended upon her explanation of why she hadn't called me until now.

"Hello Vicki," I said quietly, when she answered the telephone.

"Oh Jack. I'm glad you called me back. To be honest I wasn't sure that you would. I'm glad that you did, Jack. Really glad you did..." she said trailing off at the end.

She sounded tired or sad.

"To be honest I was a little conflicted about returning your call. I know we only had one date, but I thought that we had a good time, really hit it off, you know?" I said.

I guessed, that I was the one that sounded tired or sad, now. Either description was fairly accurate.

"I know Jack. I hope you give me a chance to explain. Can you meet me at the coffee shop on the corner, just off campus?"

I agreed to meet her, hung up the phone and began to get ready. I waffled between being excited to see her and apprehensive about what she had to say.

An hour later, I was sitting in the coffee shop. I tried to be patient but failed miserably. I checked my watch every minute or so and found that ten minutes had passed since I had gotten my coffee and began to nurse it while I waited. I had just finished checking my watch and I looked up to see Vicki smiling at me from the doorway. She held a finger up to me and then went to the counter to get herself a coffee before coming over and sitting with me. She didn't sit across from me as I expected her to, instead she sat in the booth right beside me.

My heart beat a little faster when I first saw her, and it beat like a jack hammer, now that she was beside me. She sat looking at me for some time before she started to speak.

"It's crazy. I know I don't owe you an explanation, but I want to explain. We only met for a few hours, weeks ago, but I do feel that this, you and me, is worth exploring," she said, motioning with her hand back and forth from her to me.

Then she sat quietly, searching my face with her eyes. She seemed drained from speaking.

"It's good to see you Vicki. I was starting to believe that I would never see you again. What happened? What took so long for you get back to me?"

"It's complicated, or it was. It's simple now, at least for me. You might think differently, and I wouldn't blame you. I realize that you don't owe me the time of day, but I do hope that you'll hear me out," she said quietly, took a few sips of her coffee, falling silent.

"You have my undivided attention. I just want you to know that I think that there is definitely something between us, that I would like to continue to explore. It sounds like you feel the same way," I said, turning in my seat, so that I could look directly into her eyes.

"Okay. This is hard for me to say; partly because I'm a little embarrassed and partly because I'm worried by what you might think. When we met, I was on a break from my boyfriend. You were a welcome distraction, but we got along so well, and you made me feel special in a way that I hadn't experienced in such a long time, that I really questioned my relationship more than ever. You have to understand, that there was a lot of history there and it wasn't all bad. You know? Anyway, the day after we met, he showed up at my door and professed his undying love to me and was so kind, I thought that perhaps there was a chance for us, after all. I'm not sure if I was just blind or he just put on a good act, but either way I eventually started to see cracks in his façade and now I see that we have no future together. I've been contemplating calling you for over a week, but I was too afraid. I wasn't sure what I would say to you. I decided that the truth was the only option and then let the chips fall where they may," she said, exhaling slowly, and then sat, staring at her hands.

I grabbed her hand and held it gently in mine and waited until she turned to face me.

"You don't owe me anything, but I'm glad that you explained it to me. I would very much like to pursue whatever this is, and wherever it takes us. I think that we should take it slow though. As much as I want to get to know you better, I don't want to be in a rebound relationship either. I want us both to be certain of our feelings... This all sounds a little heavy for a second date. What do you say we go for a walk in the park? It's a beautiful day."

"That sounds like a great idea, and thanks for understanding," she said, sounding relieved, and smiling warmly.

I was concerned that she had so recently broken up with her boyfriend. I wasn't worried that she would go back to him, but I was a little scared that it might be too soon for her to pursue a relationship with me. I did the one thing I could and that was to try and take it as slow as possible.

We dated for a couple of months and I tried to limit seeing her to a couple of times a week. It was certainly not because I didn't want to see her. I was addicted to her, but I stuck to my initial plan to take it slowly. Eventually, I was confident that our relationship was on solid ground and we began to see each other nearly every day. I guess I made it sound like this was my decision alone, but this was a decision that we both talked about and agreed upon.

I had never met anyone as giving, spontaneous and full of life as Vicki. I was smitten with her from the very beginning, but because of my own baggage, I was always waiting for things to go wrong. They didn't go wrong. We got closer and closer and shared many wonderful memories together. I couldn't imagine my life without her and if it weren't for bad Jack, I never would have believed that we could be separated. My resolve is firm though. I will not allow what she and I have, to be ruined by the likes of him. I will do whatever is necessary to protect her and our relationship from him.

CHAPTER TWELVE

I was running out of free time. The school year was looming large in the not too distant future. Soon, I would have to start getting ready for the new year and I wouldn't have as much time or energy to focus on dealing with bad Jack and getting my life with Vicki back on track. I was confident that Bruce and Hank could help with that, but I was going to help my own cause. It was time to jump over and go see what he was up to and confront him if need be.

I made the jump and was walking down Main street minutes later. I really had no concrete plans, but I knew that I wasn't about to back down if I came face to face with him. There was a parade advertised for the day after tomorrow. It was their Independence Day. Freedom Day, it was called here, and it was celebrated on August 25th. There were balloons and ribbons decorating the entire downtown core. It was just one of the subtle differences, between my home town and this one. I made my way up the street and took a short-cut across the park on my way to the subdivision where bad Jack lived. I got his address from the newspaper clipping with his horrible mug shot draped across the front of it. It was a miserable day. The wind howled, blowing leaves from the trees and across the grass at my feet. A light mist of rain blew sideways with the gusts of wind. I wiped my eyes continually, as I walked. There was no one in the park today. It was a lonely place, when it was deserted like it was right now. Normally it was a happy place to visit; full of laughter from children playing and love from couples walking hand in hand along the myriad of paths that snaked throughout the park. It wasn't quiet though; the wind whipping through the trees and rustling the leaves saw to that. I walked at a brisk pace, trying to get from the one side of the park and to the shelter of the houses on the other side.

I'm not sure if I heard something or if I caught something out of the corner of my eye. Whichever it was it didn't matter. What mattered, was that when I did finally turn my head, Stinky was bearing down on me at full speed, looking like a bull at full charge. I couldn't avoid being tackled by him. I was sent sprawling headlong off to my left. My side exploded with excruciating pain as two of my ribs broke under the weight of his shoulder driving me to the ground. He went sprawling past me a couple of yards across the slick grass, before righting himself, spinning around, jumping on top of me and pinning me to the ground.

"Hello asshole," he said grinning, showing his hideous mixture of missing and yellow-brown teeth.

I didn't respond, partly because I was in shock and partly because the pain in my side was overwhelming.

"Surprise! Thought you could give me the slip did ya. I wasn't an all-pro linebacker by accident, you stupid fuck. Time's up mother fucker! I'm actually glad, that you didn't uphold your end of the bargain. I could use the money, who couldn't, but what the hell, I can live without it. I will really enjoy fuckin' you up, fuckin' you up real bad. You and I are going to get re-acquainted. We'll be spending a lot of quality time together in the next few days."

"I told you I would get you your money, and I will," I said, through clenched teeth, struggling to talk through the pain and the weight of him sitting on my chest.

"Keep it! I don't want your fuckin' money. I'm more interested in seeing how much I can fuck you up, before you check out," he said, smiling sadistically.

I kept quiet. I knew there was no dissuading him from what he wanted to do. I knew my one chance was to just co-operate and not piss him off, until I could find a way to escape.

He jumped to his feet with an agility that belied his outward appearance. I knew at that moment, that I was in for a whole world of hurt. There was no way that I would be able to over-power him or outrun him either. I was fucked. He knew it and I knew it, only I was a little more concerned for my well-being than he was at the moment.

He dragged me across the park and down several back alleys. There was no one out and about today because of the foul weather, and so it was easy for him to not draw attention to us. He stopped in an alley with several dumpsters full of heaps of garbage. They filled the alley with a stench, that rivaled the smell of the man himself. He held me firmly with one hand while he produced a key from his pants pocket. He opened the door and pushed me ahead of him and into the darkness. Once inside, he let go of me and turned on the light. It was a large studio apartment.

It took a few seconds for my eyes to adjust fully from the dark of the alley, to the now brightly lit room. I was surprised by what I saw. It was a large, airy space, with high ceilings and two large industrial ceiling fans, spinning on opposite sides of the room. The apartment was clean and well furnished with modern furniture and appliances. There were several paintings adorning the walls and beautiful throw rugs placed strategically in front of the furniture and in high traffic areas.

"Make yourself comfortable," he said, as he grabbed my hands and wrenched them behind me.

He forced me into a wooden chair in front of the television. He produced some duct tape from a nearby cabinet and proceeded to wrap my wrists tightly and then attached them to the chair for good measure.

I winced in pain, as my ribs were pulled backward.

"Oh, I'm sorry. Did that hurt?" he asked, as he laughed and jabbed me in the ribs once for fun.

I gasped at the fresh, sharp pain, and Stinky laughed again with delight.

"I think I'm going to enjoy our time together," he said, then left the room and went into the bathroom.

I surveyed the room, trying to come up with an escape plan. All the windows were set high in the walls, so I ruled them out quickly. The one main window was a bit larger and more accessible, but it had bars over it. None of that mattered, as long as my hands were tied behind my back. I had to find a way to get the tape off, if I had any chance to escape. In order to make the jump back home, I needed two things. I would need to see a thin spot to access, and my hands free to rip it open. I tried to move the chair closer to the counter, in hopes that there was a knife available.

"I can hear you fuck head. Keep it up and when I'm finished here, I'm going to make you sorry," he said, in a loud but calm voice.

I stopped moving and sat with my chin on my chest, straining to come up with a plan of attack, but so far nothing came to mind. I waited for him to come back, waiting to see what my fate might be.

Stinky came back into the room and a waft of shit and urine smell flooded the room. My initial reaction was to cover my nose and mouth with my hands, but of course I forgot about my tied hands. The tape stopped their forward motion and sent a fresh stab of pain shooting through my ribs and now my wrists. He smiled at me again. It seemed that the sight of me in pain, never got old for him.

"What are we going to do with you? What happened to us, we were such good friends?" he said, threw his head back and laughed and laughed.

I was glad he was enjoying himself at my expense, but as long as he was talking to me, I thought there was a glimmer of hope, that I could reason with him.

"Listen, we can still work something out. I've been super busy, and I completely forgot about what day it was. I was planning on giving you your money, I swear. I'll make it up to you. How much do you want? I have a bit of money saved up for a rainy day, you could have that," I said, then waited for his answer.

I hoped that I didn't sound desperate because I feared that it would only encourage him.

He paused for a long time before answering. He pulled a chair from in front of the table, right up close to me, turned it backward, flung one leg over it and sat down with his chin resting on the backrest.

"I might be persuaded to change my original position, but we'll talk about that later. First we're going to have a little fun together you and me."

He leaned in really close as he spoke. I had to turn my head and hold my breath, to escape the foulness of his.

When I turned my head, I noticed that the corner of the room shimmered ever so slightly, but I couldn't examine it thoroughly before Stinky grabbed my face and turned it toward him.

"If we're to continue to get along, I'll need your undivided attention. Are we clear?"

"Crystal," I responded.

"Now, we're going to play a game, but later. I'm in no real hurry. I've been up all night and I need some shut eye. But first things first. I'm going to take you into the bathroom. I don't want you having an accident on my nice clean floor. When I wake up, we'll play our little game. I think it'll be very entertaining."

He untied me from the chair but left my hands tied together. He hoisted me from the chair with one hand and pushed me along in front of him, and into the bathroom. He unzipped my pants, pulled down my underwear and sat me down hard on the toilet.

"Just like old times eh, Jack?" he said, and left the room.

It turns out that I had to go more than I knew, but I had no way of cleaning myself afterwards. When stinky came back I lobbied to have him untie me so that I could clean up, but he would have none of it. He pulled me from the toilet, hiked up my underwear and then my pants. My underwear wasn't sitting right, and my pants were crooked, but at this point, that was the least of my worries. He led me back into the other room, sat me back in the chair, re-taped my wrists to the chair and went into his bedroom to lie down.

I was left by myself, with plenty of opportunity to plan and execute my escape. The only thing standing in my way were wraps of duct tape attaching my wrists together and to the chair, with no way to remove it. I looked desperately around the room for something that would help me cut the duct tape. There had to be something; surely his apartment wasn't child proofed. The counters were all too high to reach, and my mobility was severely limited anyway.

There was a coat flung over the chair on the other side of the table across from me. I hoped that there might be a knife in one of the pockets. I slowly and carefully wiggled my way across the floor, working my way to the other side of the table. I positioned myself in front of the coat and began the arduous task of searching each pocket for a knife or something else that might be helpful to me. The first pocket contained a half-eaten muffin and a candy bar wrapper. I threw them to the floor and continued with pocket number two. There was nothing in that pocket, and nothing in pocket number three as well. In the next pocket, I found a pack of gum. No doubt to help freshen his breath I thought, and I had to stifle a giggle in spite of the precarious predicament that I currently found myself in. The next pocket contained a blood-soaked handkerchief that I quickly dropped to the floor in disgust. I was sure I didn't want to know how the blood had gotten there. I shuddered a little and continued with my search.

From the other room, I heard a noise and froze, listening intently. My heart started to hammer in my chest. My wrists protested as did my broken ribs, against the extra blood flow. It sounded as though he was getting up, but I soon realized that he was just re-positioning himself in bed. I quickly resumed my search of his coat.

There was only one pocket left to search and I held my breath as I reached deep into the pocket to feel for its contents. My fingertips settled on a small box, that felt like it was covered in plastic. I carefully slid it from the pocket but as it pulled free, I lost my grip, and it went tumbling to the floor. I heard stirring from the other room again. I stopped and listened. Eventually, I heard the welcome sound of snores. I wiggled the chair a little to my right, to get a better look at the box that I had dropped to the floor. It was a pack of cigarettes that lie on the floor, just out of reach. Try as I might, I couldn't reach them. I picked them up with my feet, but I couldn't do anything with them from there. My hope was that there was a lighter or a package of matches hidden within. I let them fall to the floor and positioned myself in front of them. I stood up and then knelt slowly until I reached my tipping point. I fell slowly forward on my knees and my forehead came to rest on the floor. From here I leaned to my right until I fell over on my side.

The chair made a small sound as it hit the floor, but there was no movement from the other room, so I continued with what I was doing.

I opened the pack of cigarettes. I nearly cried out with excitement, when I felt the familiar shape of a lighter inside. I lit the lighter and positioned it so that I could burn the tape and free my hands. I was unable to see what I was doing, so I had to guess and hope for the best. After a few seconds, I smelled the tape burning and my excitement rose with the anticipation of freeing myself. The lighter got too hot and burned my thumb. I had no choice but to drop it to the floor. I tried to see if the tape had burned enough for me to break it. It stretched a bit but held fast.

I found the lighter and tested it to make sure it had cooled enough. It had, so I continued burning the tape on my wrists. It was difficult to find the right position to burn it and on several occasions the smell of burnt hair and flesh were added to the mix. I pressed on; it couldn't possibly take much longer. I pulled outward with my left wrist to test the strength of the tape. It stretched farther this time and pulled free. My wrists came flying apart and the lighter went hurtling into the corner of the room. The tape attached to the chair was engulfed in flame and little drops of burning glue ran down the back of the chair and pooled on the floor. Smoke drifted toward the ceiling in an acrid black trail. I lie there watching it briefly.

It was the shrill sound of the fire alarm that got me moving. My wrists and hands were a mixture of numbness, and pins and needles from having the circulation cut off for so long. My broken ribs screamed, as I tried to get to my feet.

"What the fuck!" I heard, from the other room.

That got me up and moving. I knew I couldn't stand and fight or outrun him. I moved to the corner of the room and found the thin spot that I had noticed earlier. I reached up with both hands and began to rip it open. The familiar sound of ripping cardboard and broken glass filled the apartment, joined by the roar of a now wide-awake madman, that charged toward me at full speed.

I slipped through to the other side and fell headlong into a dark alley. I had a split second to revel in my successful escape, before nearly being crushed by the hulky linebacker, that had also jumped through the opening.

Thankfully, he landed on my back and on my side without the broken ribs, but he knocked the wind out of me nevertheless. I rolled over onto my back and gasped for breath, but none came. Stinky jumped to his feet and stood over me, a wild look of dis-belief evident on his face. He was a man used to having his own way and on his terms. This definitely put him out of his comfort zone.

"What the fuck is this? Where am I? he said, his mouth open in awe.

He was shaking his head back and forth, breathing heavily as he did.

I was beginning to breathe normally again. I was scrambling to come up with a new game plan. For the briefest, fleeting moment, I thought that I had escaped unscathed, except for a couple burns on my wrist and a couple of broken ribs, but otherwise not too bad really. I didn't realize that he had jumped as well.

Now I had to deal with him again, only this time, I had the fact that he was out of his element on my side.

"Welcome to my world," I said, as I got to my feet.

"I don't understand, what just happened," he said, still shaking his head.

I was in no mood to help this son of a bitch understand anything, and I didn't give a fuck what he thought or felt. I just wanted to be away from him, go home, clean up and go to bed.

"Where you goin'? I'm not finished with you yet?" he said half-heartedly, following after me, like a lost puppy.

Apparently, his priorities had changed. He was more concerned with what the fuck had just happened to him, where he was, and how to get back.

"I'm going home and you're not coming," I said, as I walked out onto the street and hailed a cab.

He stood for a moment trying to figure out his next move. By the time he righted himself, I was climbing into the back of a cab. I looked out the back window and saw him running after the cab for a few seconds, before he came to a stop in the middle of the road. He reminded me of a lost child, standing in the road, with his face downcast. I felt sorry for him, for the briefest moment, before I started to think of what I had just been through.

"Fuck him, see how he likes that," I mumbled.

"What's that buddy?" the cabbie asked.

"Nothing, just talking out loud."

The rest of the short ride home was in silence. I was tired, and the cabbie remained quiet, probably tired from a long shift. I was never so glad in all my life, to see the front steps to my house. I paid him, went inside and straight to bed. It never even occurred to me, to get out of my dirty clothes. It had been an extraordinarily long and trying day.

CHAPTER THIRTEEN

I awoke refreshed. It wasn't until I went to get up, that I remembered my broken ribs. I should say that they reminded me. My wrists hurt as well, and when I finally got to a seated position in bed, I bent down to have a better look at them. There were large blisters on both, and the surrounding skin was red.

My ribs hurt like hell and it was hard to take a full breath. They hurt more today, than they did yesterday.

I got dressed with some difficulty. I ate breakfast, then it was off to the hospital. Thankfully, it wasn't very busy, and I was in and out in three hours. Turns out my wrists weren't infected, but the doc gave me some antibiotics, to make sure that they stayed that way. A nurse wrapped them and instructed me on how to take care of them. They did x-rays to check my ribs and found out that they were cracked but not completely broken. That was good news. That meant no chance of them being dislocated and the less recovery time was a bonus.

Now the hospital visit was out of the way. I still wanted to go see bad Jack, but I was a little more concerned, because of my sore ribs. Yesterday, I was willing to do whatever, even if that meant confronting him, but now I wasn't so sure that it would be a good idea. I wanted to be pain-free, in case I was face to face with him and things didn't go according to plan. I was tired of making plans, thinking about doing things and never accomplishing anything.

I came up with a plan. I'm not saying it was necessarily a good plan, but it was a plan nevertheless. I decided to see if I could kill two birds with one stone, as they say. Stinky may not have believed me before, about me not being the Jack he knew, but I was betting that he may be a little more open to the idea now. The problem was, that I had no idea where to find him. My idea was to start where I left him and search from there, but not without a weapon.

I went to see my friend Albert. Albert lived just a couple of doors down, and he was one of those rare people that didn't have to know every bit of a person's business. He figured if you wanted him to know, then you would tell him.

"Hi Albert. How's it going?" I asked, when he opened the door.

"Not bad, haven't seen you in a while. Come in, come in, sit," he said, cheerfully.

"I've been extremely busy. You wouldn't believe me if I told you. Things have been unbelievable lately."

"Aren't you still on holidays?

"Yeah, but it's more my personal life that's been all over the place."

"Can I help somehow? Say, do you want a drink or something?"

"You can help, yes, but no, I don't need a drink, thanks."

"Okay, so how can I help?" he asked, leaning forward in his chair.

"Well... this may seem a little odd, but I need to borrow a gun. Relax, I'm not going to shoot someone or rob any banks; I just need it for protection, that's all."

"You know that's an awfully odd request coming from you. I haven't seen you for a while, and then you show up at my door asking for a gun. I don't normally stick my nose into other people's business and I'm not about to start now. I trust you Jack but are you sure there isn't anything else I can do to help?" he said, rubbing his chin, a concerned look on his face.

"I promise you, I'm not up to no good, I just need it for protection. I don't really think I'll need it, but I just want to be safe, rather than sorry."

"Okay, I trust you. You ever shot a gun before?" he asked, dubiously.

"Yeah. I was a pretty good shot too. My uncle used to let me shoot his, whenever we would go visit him. It's been a few years, but like I said, I have no desire to use it and I don't anticipate any trouble. It's just my insurance policy."

"If you don't anticipate any trouble, then why the gun? On second thought, never mind. I'll go get the gun but do me a favour and be careful."

He returned a few minutes later with a gun, a holster and a box of ammunition.

"Thanks Albert. I really appreciate it. No need for all the ammo though. I just need what's in the magazine, and like I said, I'm pretty sure I won't even need that."

He showed me how to load and unload it, and how to put the safety on and off, then handed it to me, without saying a word.

"Thanks again Albert, maybe someday when I have more time, I'll fill you in on what's going on."

"No need. Just be safe, okay," he said, and clapped me on the shoulder.

I left Albert's place and went downtown where I last saw Stinky. My plan was to check a couple of the local bars, the soup kitchen and finally the homeless shelter. My first stop was O'Malley's, a popular Irish pub right on the corner from where I last saw Stinky. I entered and approached the bar and took a look around, but there were just a couple of older gentlemen sitting there, nursing their respective beers. I asked the bartender if he had seen anyone matching Stinky's description, but he hadn't, so I thanked him and proceeded to the next bar.

Apparently, he was more resourceful than I gave him credit for. My phone was ringing so I dug it out of my back pocket and answered it.

"Hi Jack, It's your Mother. There's an old friend of yours here. He says he's known you for years, says you're really close. I don't ever remember you telling me about anyone that matches his description."

Then she whispered. "He looks a little rough around the edges, and he smells, a lot."

"I'm on my way Mom. Is Dad there?" I asked, trying to sound calm.

"Why, yes he is. Do you want me to get him?"

"No, it's okay. I'll be there in a few minutes."

I hung up the phone and felt for the gun underneath my coat. Its comforting shape hung above my ribs on the side that didn't hurt. I hurried as fast as I could, in the direction of my parents' house.

When I got there, Stinky was standing out front with a smoke in his mouth, searching his pockets looking for a lighter. I had to chuckle a little to myself.

"You have a light? I can't seem to find mine," he asked.

"No, don't smoke. What are you doing here?"

"What did you expect me to do? I don't know where the hell I am."

"We need to get something straight. I didn't bother trying to explain it before, because I never thought in a million years that you would believe me. I'm thinking that under the circumstances, you might be a little more open to what I have to tell you."

"Where the hell am I, and how the hell did we get here?"

"Well that's what we have to talk about. See this place is a twin of where you live, an alternate reality or universe if you will. Where you live, there is the Jack that you know and I'm from here. I never met you before last week, but at the time I never thought that you would ever believe me. Your beef is with him, not me."

"I kinda figured that much. I thought there was something a bit off about you, but I couldn't quite put my finger on it. I guess I owe you an apology, and if you don't mind, I'd kinda like to go home. I'll have to make a point of catching up with the Jack that I do know. I have to say, you're a dead ringer for him, you could be his twin. Sure, had me fooled."

"Yeah, I know, but looks are the only thing we have in common."

"No hard feelings I hope," he said, holding his hand out for me to shake.

I shook his hand gladly. I couldn't have hoped for the conversation to go any better than it did. I couldn't believe that I was shaking the hand of the man, that hours ago, had broken my ribs and had me tied up in his apartment.

"I understand, under the circumstances. No hard feelings. We have one thing in common, that neither of us really care for the other Jack. Somehow, I think that our paths will cross again, only next time, I sure hope it's under different circumstances," I said, laughing a little.

"Just let me say bye to my parents. Then we can shove off."

"Yeah no problem. Nice lady your Mom. Ask her if she has a lighter or some matches, will you. I'm dying for a smoke. It's been one hell of a day. You know what I mean?"

"I sure do," I said laughing.

I went in the house and did my best avoiding Mom's questions. She would have to wait until another day. I grabbed a pack of matches on the way out the door and flung them at Stinky. He snatched them out of the air with the agility of a cat.

He held out his hand.

"We haven't been formally introduced. My name's George, George Vanwall."

"Pleased to meet you George," I said, shaking his hand again.

My hand disappeared into his, like a child's hand would disappear into that of an adult's. I was sure glad, that at that moment I didn't count him among one of my enemies. I didn't count him as one of my friends just yet, but it was still a relief that I wouldn't be looking over my shoulder, worrying about when I might bump into him again.

I took George to the first available out of the way thin spot that I could find. He had a lot of questions of course, about how it worked. I answered them patiently and then helped him through the opening. He was like a kid on Christmas morning. He was so excited, and the smile on his face was truly from ear to ear. He slid through, the world closed in behind him, and he was gone. Considering how my luck had been going lately, that encounter couldn't possibly have gone any better. I was smiling to myself as I turned the corner and headed back to Albert's house to return his gun.

The phone in my back pocket started to ring again. I pulled it out and looked at it. I thought about not answering it for a moment, but then decided to go ahead anyway. After the string of bad luck I was having, it was unlikely to be more bad news.

"Jack, is that you?" he asked.

I could tell it was Hank right away. He had a very distinctive voice. It was quiet and a little raspy. I knew that my hopes of having no bad news, were dashed.

"Hey Hank, what's up?" I asked, worriedly.

"My boy just called me. Bad Jack is downtown as we speak. He's been poking around by the office building where Vicki works."

"He's there right now?"

"Yeah, he just called me a minute ago."

"Okay, thanks. I'm going down there."

"I wouldn't do that if I were you. My boy's got it covered. Right now, you have the element of surprise. Why don't you use this opportunity to go do some reconnaissance of your own back at his place?"

"You know, that's not such a bad idea. Okay, thanks Hank."

"Let me know what you find out. Keep me posted."

"Will do, and thanks again Hank."

"Don't mention it, take care," he said and hung up.

I walked the few steps back to where I had helped Stinky, or George, go to the other side. I opened the hole and went through myself. I headed toward the park, to take the short-cut that I started to take the other day, before George had to go and ruin my plans.

Minutes later, I was standing in front of bad Jack's house. I went around back of the house to try and get a look inside, without drawing attention to myself. Apparently, someone had beaten me to it. I was guessing that that someone was probably George. The screen door was slightly open, and the back door was as well. Whoever had gained access, didn't bother to close the door when they left. I peered through the large window at the back, shielding my eyes from the sun to see into the darkness. It didn't appear as though anyone was still inside. I found it to be a little creepy, but I decided to go in and take a quick look around. It was a small two-bedroom bungalow. The floors were covered in wall to wall carpets and they were stained dark where the high traffic areas were. There was evidence everywhere, that someone had been looking for something. Drawers were left open, the cushions on the couch and loveseat were strewn about the living room. Kitchen cupboards were ajar and the mattresses on the beds were sitting slightly askew. There were papers and boxes littering the floor. I didn't want to press my luck and venture into the basement, but I did take a quick look in all the upstairs rooms. There was nothing to see in the bathroom and I had already seen the bedrooms and the living room. The last one appeared to be a computer room or den. There was a computer on the desk, that had been left on and all the drawers had been ransacked. The rest I paid no attention to because my eyes never left the wall, to the left of the computer desk. There on the wall, in perfectly formed rows, were row upon row of pictures of me, Vicki, my Mom, Dad and Helen, Jason and the kids. A shiver ran up my spine. How creepy was this, to find pictures of all my family members on his wall? My first reaction was to rip them all from the wall, but I didn't want him to know that I had been here. Something told me that he would find out soon enough, who had ransacked his house, but until then I wanted to fly under the radar. I felt suddenly ill. I needed to get out of there, to get as far away from this place as possible. I had to tell Hank and Bruce what I found, so that they knew the seriousness of the situation.

He obviously spent a fair amount of time thinking about me and my family and doing his research. Then I got to thinking; I hated how my mind worked sometimes. When it came down to it, were we really all that different, after all? I had been as pre-occupied with him and his family as he had been with mine. The difference was that I had no ill-will toward his family and I couldn't say the same for him. I'd still like to believe that I was nothing like him. It's funny how I could despise someone so much, someone that I had never met. I have my Grandma to thank for that I guess; that and the fact that he just happened to be a serial sex offender. I just needed to get out of here. The negative energy from this place was starting to affect me, and I knew just the place to go, to get cheered up.

I knocked twice on the door and waited. I put my ear to the door to hear if he was stirring inside. Nothing, so I knocked again, louder.

"Don't get your panties in a bunch. I'm coming, I'm coming," Bruce called from behind the door.

He flung the door open and turned to walk back inside. I followed him into his study and he motioned for me to have a seat. He continued toward the sink. He washed his face with cold water and then dried it off and sat down in his recliner.

"Had a few drinks with the boys last night, and this morning. I think I might be getting too old for this, I would say. Just give me a minute to collect myself," he said, then got up and turned on the coffee maker.

"Would you like one?" he asked.

"Sure, I'll have one. Two sugars, one milk please."

He came back and sat in his recliner.

"Sure. You can get it when it's ready. I'll take mine black, please," he said, lying back and closing his eyes.

He sat there with his eyes closed, not speaking. I started to wonder if he had fallen asleep. When the coffee was ready, I went and made mine and got his as well. I set mine on the table and handed his to him. As it got close to him and he smelled the aroma of it, he sat up immediately, inhaled deeply and grabbed hold of the cup. He held the cup as though it was the most valuable thing imaginable. He sipped at his coffee without saying a word. He drank about half of it before he started to look a little more animated. When he was nearly finished, he began to act like his old self.

"Nothing like that first coffee in the morning to get you going, I would say, or in this case the afternoon. What brings you by my boy?"

"I'll just cut right to it. I was just at bad Jack's house and I was snooping around. It seems that he has been doing an awful lot of homework on me and my family. I found a wall in his den with pictures of us all over it."

"Wait. What! You were inside of his house? Why? How?" he asked.

"It's complicated, but I knew from Hank that he wasn't home, so I went to do some reconnaissance. His house had been ransacked before I got there. So, I let myself in to have a look around. It's worse than I thought. He had pictures of me and Vicki, my Mom and Dad, Helen, Jason and the kids. He's been busy. I'm not sure what he's up to, but I can tell you, I don't like it."

"I have to agree with you there. I don't like it one little bit either. I have Hank looking after things on your side, perhaps it's time I get someone over here to keep tabs on him," he said, thoughtfully. "If they aren't already," he mumbled under his breath.

Jack didn't hear him, and he paid it no attention. By now, he was used to the Professors mumblings and he never gave it a second thought.

"It couldn't hurt, although I have a feeling that he may find himself in a spot of trouble, in the not too distant future. I'm not sure if I told you about Stinky or not, actually his name is George. I can't remember anything these days, it's been such a blur these last few days and weeks. Anyway, bad Jack owes him money. I think he ransacked his place, and I can tell you, he's one dude that you don't want to cross. If he runs into him, he's in for a world of hurt."

"Well that's too bad for him, but that plays right into our hands, I would say."

"I agree, but I would still feel better if we had someone watching him over here."

"Yeah, yeah, I agree whole-heartedly. Better to be safe than sorry, I would say. I'll get right on that, right after we are done eating. Come on, I'm taking you to one of my favourite places, and I'm not taking no for an answer," he said, bouncing from his chair.

I went out to eat with Bruce and the food was awesome, as was the company. He always had a way of cheering me up and taking my thoughts from my troubles, if only for the short time that we were together.

The day certainly ended a lot better than it had begun. Perhaps things were starting to go my way for a change.

CHAPTER FOURTEEN

I went to bed that night in a positive frame of mind. Despite what I had found at bad Jack's house. My ribs felt much better, barely hurt in fact. I was confident that I had turned a corner and that things would start to get better. We had Hank's buddy watching out for him here and Bruce was going to get someone to do the same over there. Stinky, or George I should say, would hopefully take care of him for me. Things were looking up. All I had to do now, was to get Vicki back into my life and things would be right again...

I hadn't thought about Henry Johnson in a long time but when I fell asleep, I dreamt about him that night.

"Be careful Jack, I know what kind of cold heart, that bad Jack of yours has. I know because my brother has a cold heart too."

He spoke quietly, almost whispering, as if he didn't want his brother to hear, even though his brother was nowhere to be seen. He looked around and then cupped his hands in front of his mouth. He looked sad, forlorn. I felt for him and a little for me as well. I missed Henry. I think he was a good soul; he was just misguided by his brother.

"You have to stop him. I should have stopped my brother, but I didn't have the courage," he said, sullenly.

I tried to tell him that I was sorry for what happened to him, but he turned and walked away, without saying another word.

When I awoke the following morning, my thoughts drifted immediately to Henry. He appeared to be so sad in my dream and my heart ached for him. He died so young and at a time when he was finally trying to break free from his brother's influence. My thoughts inevitably turned to Billy.

For quite a while after Henry's death. Billy Johnson was sullen and withdrawn. He wouldn't even look at me or give me the time of day. I liked the fact that he left me alone, but when he did, I thought of Henry and the way he had helped me the last time I had seen him alive. I didn't realize until many years later, how profound an effect the Johnson boys had made on my life. I thought many times about him in the days and weeks after his death and obviously, even now, I still think about him on occasion.

I wouldn't say that he avoided me, but he certainly didn't go out of his way to bully me like he did. There was the odd verbal jab thrown in my direction, but that was about it, until six months later. I think maybe I reminded him too much of the time that Henry stood up to him, or perhaps it was because he didn't have him to show off for anymore. What the reason was, I'm not certain, but he did leave me alone for a while, and then out of the blue, he decided to have another go at me.

Billy was sitting on the bridge one morning. The very same bridge that he had tormented me on that day, years before. I thought at first that he was just going to watch me walk past without saying anything. I think that maybe he was going to, but sometimes with Billy it was as if a switch clicked on or off, and he went off for no particular reason. This incident was different than any other I had experienced before. I caught a glimpse into just how troubled he really was, but of course I didn't fully understand how truly troubled he was, until years later.

"You know, it's your fault that he's dead," he said quietly, as he jumped from the side of the bridge.

I just ignored him and kept walking. It took me several seconds to piece together what he had said. He said it so quietly, that at first, I wasn't sure.

He stood in front of me with his eyes cast to the ground. He reminded me of Henry, standing that way. I nearly felt sorry for him, then I remembered, that this was not Henry. He was nothing like his brother, except for the family resemblance.

"It should have been you that was killed. I would have enjoyed that. I hate it when people make me do things I don't want to do. I like doing things because I want to do them. It's better that way. It feels better. It fills me up," he said, still looking at the ground.

I stopped walking and stood about ten yards ahead of him in the middle of the path. I wasn't sure exactly what he was talking about, but I kind of read between the lines. Billy no longer scared me like he had before. I had grown considerably since that first encounter and he had remained roughly the same size. It was his demeanor that I felt troubling. I said nothing and waited for him to speak again.

He just stood looking at the ground. I couldn't see his face, but based on his actions, I could tell that he was crying. He wiped one eye with the back of his hand and then the other, sniffling as he did. Eventually he fell to his knees and began to sob.

I stood motionless. I wasn't sure what to do, but after several seconds I started walking again. He began to speak, louder this time.

"Usually it fills me up," he began.

This was the second time he said something about filling him up, and again, I had no idea what he was talking about.

"I thought it would fill me up. It's the first time that it didn't. I have an idea why it didn't. Pretty sure why anyhow. I'm still learning, but I'm willing to practice until I get it right," he said, looking up for the first time, an evil grin spreading across his face.

"Well, have fun with that," I said, and started to move past him.

He jumped from his knees with all the agility that I had experienced on several occasions before. He was like a cat or a cobra, springing into action. I was impressed, in spite of myself, by the quickness and fluidity of his movements. Before I had any chance of escape, he was behind me, his arm wrapped around me, with what felt like the sharp point of a knife held to my throat.

"This is for Henry. You're going to help fill me up. We'll have to go farther into the woods, because it's going to take a while."

Now, there was no doubt that Billy was faster than me by a long shot, but I was bigger and stronger than him. I also had the element of surprise, and his over-confidence working against him. I waited until he loosened his grip on me and shoved me ahead of him. His plan was to lead me into the forest and by the sounds of it he planned on torturing me. I had a different idea about what we were going to do. I saw Henry stand up to him and now it was my turn. I remembered how surprised Billy was on that day long ago and now I wanted to see that same look on his face. I turned to face him and started to plead with him. He thought that I was scared, and this delighted him. He threw back his head and laughed with delight. This is for Henry sure enough, I thought, as I drove my right foot up as hard as I could between his legs. He stopped laughing in a hurry and the look of delight was replaced with shock and horror. He fell over on his side and writhed in pain. I wasted no time... and this is for me, I thought, as I kicked him hard in the side of the face. His knife fell from his limp hand and I reached down to pick it up. I stood over him for a moment, looking down at him. I was relieved by the outcome of course but thought that I would have taken more pleasure in finally besting my nemesis. Instead, I found myself wondering what could have made Billy the way he was. What happened to him to make him so unhappy, so evil? I guess that's what made me different from him. I took no real pleasure in what I had just done. I knelt beside him and checked that he was breathing. He stirred a little as I did. I stood up, threw the knife into the woods as far as possible, turned and continued on my way, along the path.

That was the last time I had any problems with Billy Johnson. In fact, shortly after that he quit school and moved away.

It should have been a liberating feeling, but I didn't know then, that the days of Billy trying to bully me were over. I continued to look over my shoulder waiting for him to try again, until he moved away.

I went to bed in a positive mood but my dream about Henry and subsequent trip down memory lane had spoiled that. I was interested in getting back to that place. The positive place, that is.

Vicki always knew how to cheer me up. I desperately wanted to see her. I had no doubt that she would know exactly what to say.

When we were dating she always had new and exciting things planned for us. The excitement of being in a new relationship helped of course, but that was only part of it. We always found the time to be together, to do things.

There were so many good experiences, memories. I paused to think, and all the memories flooded through my thoughts. So many, that I had a hard time keeping them straight in my head.

There was the time we went to an amusement park. It started out cloudy that day but before we knew it, the rain was coming down in waves. Most of the thrill seekers were running for cover but Vicki convinced me to stay with her and continue to go on the rides. We went on ride after ride without being hampered by waiting in lines. When one ride was over we immediately got onto the next ride, and so on. We had an amazing time, on a day that I probably would have run to the hills with the rest of the people, if not for her urging me to stay.

We went sky-diving, we've been diving in the ocean. We've ridden horses and drove dune buggies. We've attended weddings together and struggled through funerals together. We've seen our friends start new relationships and watched others end theirs. We've seen births and baptisms and graduations together. Through all of this, we remained close and for the most part happy. That is of course until bad Jack came calling, But, he doesn't know the bond that we share. We can overcome anything together, and when this is all over, we will add our wedding to the long list of our accomplishments. I'm sure of it.

Enough pussy-footing around. I decided to go see Vicki and explain to her, what's been happening and take back control of my life, once and for all.

I took a few minutes to shave and throw on something decent. It had been awhile since I had seen her, and I wanted to look good. I was a little nervous as I left the house; partly because I wasn't sure how she would react to me showing up at her work and partly because I really missed her. I walked out the door and headed downtown. I was hopeful that she wouldn't be too upset with me. I had mixed feelings about how she'd receive me, but it was time that she knew the whole truth.

As I approached the building where she worked I became more nervous. I wiped my hands on my pants, to remove the sweat. I reached out to grasp the handle of the front door, but I caught something out of the corner of my eye. The entrance to her building was constructed entirely of glass. The main foyer was two stories tall and the entire thing was made of glass as well. It wasn't unusual to see lots of people milling about inside and on the sidewalk in front of the building. The effect was enhanced by the glass. I could see everyone on the first level, inside the building and out. This was a little disorienting at first, because some of the people's reflections from outside were added to the mix.

I turned my head to see what had caught my eye. At first glance, I nearly dismissed it as my own reflection. I was seeing what looked like my reflection, but the clothes were all wrong. Bad Jack. That all too familiar feeling of ice running down my spine, happened again. His hair was cut to match mine. He was wearing blue jeans and a T-shirt, that matched ones that I had at home. He was staring directly at me. After a second or so, that felt more like minutes, he smiled at me. It was more of a smirk at first, but it slowly morphed into a crooked smile that spread across his face. The same terrible smile, that I had until this moment, only seen in pictures.

He was standing on the other side of the main entrance and there was a pane of glass between us. He turned to his left and walked around to the front of the building and stopped a couple of feet from me.

"So, we finally meet in person. I feel like we've known each other for years. I feel like sometimes I'm not sure where I stop, and you begin. You know what I mean?" he said, smiling the entire time.

But it wasn't a friendly smile. It was a smug, condescending smile.

I wanted to wipe that sickening smile from his face. I had for many years wondered what I would say to him, if we ever came face to face. Well, here I was, and I was at a loss for words.

"You here to visit Vicki? She's a good one, should hang on to that one. I wouldn't let her out of your sight if I were you," he said, still smiling.

"I will, you can be sure of that."

The spell had been broken, when he began to talk about Vicki. I may not stand up for myself as much as I should, but I would die for her.

He continued to talk as though I had said nothing.

"Yeah she's one in a million. She has the looks, personality, brains; the whole package. I'm a little jealous, I don't mind admitting. What I wouldn't do, to be with a woman like that."

"Let's get one thing crystal clear. I don't want you anywhere near her, you hear me?"

"Don't worry Jack. We're friends, right? I just want what's best for you. What's best for you is best for me, right? Besides sometimes we only think we know what we want. Isn't that right?" he asked, still smiling, always smiling

"I know just as much about you, as you know about me, so you can drop the act," I said.

His smile was gone now. He took a step forward, so that he was nice and close. He whispered in my ear, and then took a step back.

"Better be careful Jacky boy. Just two guys having a friendly chat here, that's all. I don't want you to misunderstand me. I'm not the bad guy here. I want out of life what I deserve. That's all, nothing more, nothing less. Anyway, I gotta run but it's sure been nice talking to you. We'll do it again real soon, I promise," he said, as he turned quickly and walked in the other direction.

I thought it was strange that he ended the conversation so abruptly. I turned toward the door to go in and I realized why.

"Hi Vicki," I said, when I saw her walking toward me.

"What are you doing here? I told you yesterday, that I still need some space."

"I need to talk to you or more show you something, I guess. I wouldn't ask if it wasn't important. I know you need more time and I respect that, but I think you'll understand when I show you."

"Okay Jack. I'm free tomorrow."

"Can it be tonight? It's pretty important." I asked.

"I'm swamped tonight; tomorrow."

"Tomorrow's fine. I'll pick you up around 7 if that's okay?"

"I'll see you tomorrow Jack. This had better be good, or it's just going to push me further away. I don't want any games," she said, sounding tired.

"No games, I promise. You'll understand when I show you. I'll see you tomorrow. I love you Vicki."

"Okay tomorrow then. I love you too, that was never the problem," she said, and kept walking.

At least she agreed to meet me, which was great news. She would understand everything tomorrow. I was sure that she would feel differently, when she knew the truth. What I didn't see was bad Jack standing just around the corner, listening to the entire conversation.

I went home after that and despite the conversation I had had with bad Jack; I felt awesome, almost giddy. For the last couple days, things had started to go my way. Vicki had agreed to meet me, and I couldn't be happier. I knew that she'd be blown away by my news, and once she heard the rest of the story; I knew that she would forgive me. She'd undoubtedly think it was incredibly cool, to be able to jump.

It was difficult to contain my excitement; hard to do anything but think about Vicki and how I was going to show her and what I was going to tell her. The minutes seemed to drag by like the hands on the clock were stuck. I watched a movie, and that helped to distract me for a while. My thoughts kept wandering, and several times I had to rewind the movie, to catch parts that I had missed. Eventually it was time for bed, and I welcomed the chance to be free from my thoughts, for the next eight hours or so.

I lie there looking at the ceiling for probably a half hour, and I was still awake.

"Be careful of that one Jack," a voice said, from the dark room.

I reached over to my nightstand to turn on the light, but nothing happened. My heart rate rose, but I lie still, waiting for the person to speak again. The room gradually became lighter and lighter, until I was able to make out the silhouette of a person standing in the corner. The room continued to lighten, and the walls began to fade away. They were replaced with green grass and trees. A dirt path snaked its way away from my bed, for as far as I could see. It was light enough now, to see that the figure that was standing on the path in front of me, was Henry Johnson. I stood on the path, several yards in front of him, his eyes downcast, kicking at some pebbles with his shoe. He raised his head to look at me and smiled when he saw me. It was a warm, genuine smile, so unlike bad Jack's smile that I had encountered earlier in the day.

"What's up Henry?" I asked, trying to lighten the mood.

He looked back down at his shoes and began to kick at the pebbles, before looking up again. He smiled, and the sadness drained from his face.

"I like you Jack. You're one of the few people that could understand me, understand what I've been through. I guess we're kindred spirits," he said, laughing at his reference to spirit.

"I like you too. I wish it hadn't been this way."

"Yeah, me too, obviously," he said, waving his hand through his midsection, to prove his point.

"What brings you by Henry?"

"I get lonely, that and I wanted to warn you about bad Jack. He's up to no good. I think he's plannin' something bad for you. I just had a feelin' that's all. Sometimes that's all we got to go on, is our gut," he said, before the light of the room slowly faded, and was replaced by the darkness.

I looked over the end of the bed toward the door where Henry had been standing moments earlier. The dream seemed so real, that I half-expected him to be there. I jumped a little, when I saw what looked like a figure standing there. I relaxed ever so slightly. I knew it couldn't be Henry. He wasn't haunting me; it was just a dream. Then from the darkness, the figure took a step forward.

"Hello Jack," he said, his crooked grin appearing more grotesque than ever, caught in the moonlight seeping through the blind and into my room.

My heart started pounding wildly in my chest and I started to sit up. Before I could, he moved forward quickly. The moonlight glinted off metal in his right hand. As he lifted it, I clearly saw the shape of a gun.

"I knew we'd be seeing each other real soon, but this is sooner than even I had anticipated. I want to make myself real clear. I have no problem killing you, if that's the way it plays out, but that's not my motivation here. I thought I wanted your life, but it turns out that your life isn't so great after all. Vicki on the other hand, well, now that's something different. I think she will be much happier with me, than with you."

"If you touch her, I'll kill you!" I yelled.

"Now Jack, I hardly think that you're in any position to make threats. Maybe you should just lie back and relax. I brought a knife too just in case you preferred that, but don't worry I won't use it unless you ask me to," he said, pulling a large knife out of a sheath from beneath his pant leg.

"So, what's your plan then? What are you going to do with me?"

"To be honest, I haven't figured that part out. I'll have to get back to you on that, but in the meantime, I want to know where I can find you, when I need to," he said, pulling a roll of duct tape from his coat pocket and walking over to the side of the bed.

"I would encourage you to cooperate at this point, in order to avoid any further complications," he said, pausing, shaking his head and then continuing,

"Is this as surreal an experience for you as it is for me? I mean, it really is like looking into a mirror."

I didn't respond. I was too busy trying to form a plan of escape, too busy trying to figure out what he was up to. Yeah, it was a surreal experience by the way. This was the second time this week that I was about to be tied up by a madman, that may or may not kill me. So yeah, it was a surreal experience, thank you very much for asking! I thought.

Bad Jack, on the other hand, seemed to be having a grand old time; smiling and whistling as he worked. He wrenched my hands behind my back and then duct taped them together. He made me lie on my stomach and tied my feet to the footboard. Then he stood at the end of my bed, looking at me, admiring his handiwork, a smug grin on his face.

"Well, I can't stand around all day. As much as I enjoy visiting with you; I do have things to do. I have to find some nice clothes to wear, for my big date tonight. I might clean your car out and wash it. I hope there's gas in it. By the way, where are the keys?" he asked, in an upbeat, happy tone.

I wasn't about to play along. I remained silent.

"That's okay, I understand you don't feel much like talking. I won't take it personal. You have a lot on your plate at the moment. I understand," he said, mocking me.

I wouldn't have thought it possible that I could hate someone as much as I hated him. I really didn't like the way he made me feel. I had never thought about hurting another person in my entire life; not even Billy Johnson. I think my saving grace was that I didn't want to be like either of them. I would continue to take the high road and let karma take care of the rest. I wasn't afraid anymore for my own safety, but I was deathly afraid of what he might do to Vicki, and I saw no way for me to help her.

Bad Jack went to the closet and got out some shirts and then rummaged through my dresser, trying to find a pair of pants to go with them. He held each piece of clothing up, looking in the mirror, deciding if he liked it or not. Then he turned to face me, to ask for my approval. I didn't answer him of course. Undaunted, he replayed the same scenario over and over again. He was enjoying every minute of it, savouring every second.

He grabbed some socks from the top drawer, placed them all on the bed and left the room. He returned moments later with a pair of shoes, that he had retrieved from the mat near the front door. He was also carrying a couple of pictures, that had been hung on the wall in the entrance way. He placed the pictures on the dresser facing me, so he was able to see them as he sorted through the piles of clothes on my bed.

"I couldn't decide what to wear, too many choices and I didn't like any of them, so I decided to let you and Vicki decide for me. I figured she would believe it was you, even more if I was dressed in your clothes, ones that she had seen before. Of course, you're going to let me borrow your car, which I think is awfully considerate of you. What do you say we see what they look like on me, shall we?" he said, smugly.

He undressed and started to dress himself in my clothes. I had to bite my tongue to prevent myself from unleashing a tirade of profanity. I knew that it would only serve to buoy his spirits even further, and I had had enough of his bullshit already. I wanted him to be gone as quickly as possible, so that I could get to work on trying to escape.

He finished dressing, did one final check in the mirror and spun once for me, for good measure. He then went into the kitchen, where I could hear him moving things around in the refrigerator. I figured he was looking for something to eat, but I underestimated how his mind worked.

"Attention to detail, that's the trick," he said smiling, holding one of my beers in his hand.

He stood looking at me for a minute, not saying anything. He opened the beer and finished it in three swallows. He wiped his mouth with the back of his hand. His large, creepy, twisted grin spread across his face again.

"Wow! That's great beer. Better than anything we have at home. I'll be sure to order one at dinner. Say, what's Vicki's favourite restaurant? You know what, never mind. I'll take her somewhere new. I think it's best if we make our own memories together."

I remained silent. I wanted so badly to scream at the top of my lungs, but I needed him to just finish taunting me and leave even more. I finally got my wish.

"Well, I hate to run, but I have to go home and clean up a bit before my big date. You just lie back and relax. I'll come back and visit; if not tonight then first thing tomorrow morning. Oh, and if you're looking for your wallet, don't worry, I have it. Have a good day, I know I will. I'm just going to take your car now, if that's alright? I don't want to come back later. If things go as well as I hope they will. I'll be busy. If you know what I mean," he said, winking, and then had a good laugh, at my expense.

That's okay, I thought. We'll see who has the last laugh.

CHAPTER FIFTEEN

He left, and I immediately got to work trying to free myself. I tried my hands first, but they were bound together with my palms facing one another and I couldn't move them at all. I stopped to think for a minute. I always found, it was better to work smarter, rather than harder. Maybe if I just thought about it for a minute, something might come to me.

The phone was too far away for me to reach and I didn't have anything in my pockets that would help me cut myself free. I didn't have a lighter either, I thought. That made me laugh a bit despite my present predicament. I didn't want to struggle too much or twist the duct tape. That would only serve to make the duct tape stronger. My best chance of escape was to have the tape remain flat and therefore easier to rip.

I once worked with a guy that ripped a phone book in half with his bare hands. The book was 4 inches thick and my hands could barely grasp the covers, let alone rip the book in half. The first time I saw it done I was amazed by the sheer strength of the man. He was a large man for sure, but that wasn't what enabled him to perform this seemingly impossible feat. The second time he showed me, how he accomplished it. He twisted the pages back and forth in a sawing motion, ripping several pages at once and not the whole book.

I looked at my present situation in much the same way. If I was able to rip a few fibres at a time, then eventually I would be free of my restraints. The only real hope I had was my feet. My hands were a lost cause as far as I could tell. My ankles were taped together and then fastened to the footboard of the bed. There was enough room for me to move my legs and feet, but I wanted to be careful not to roll the tape over on itself, thereby making it stronger.

I carefully moved my legs back and forth, trying to rip the duct tape. The layers of tape were too thick to make any real progress, but I pressed on, until eventually I had to face the fact that I was getting nowhere.

I knew time wasn't on my side. I looked to the small alarm clock on my nightstand and was horrified to see that it was now 6:30 p.m. Where did the day go? He was going to pick her up at 7 and I wanted to be there before that happened.

I gave up trying to be patient and working at my restraints methodically. I started kicking my feet and thrashing wildly on my bed, and still the duct tape held. I was out of breath now and sweating profusely. I took a minute to catch my breath and allow my heart rate to return to normal. I took a few seconds to mutter some swear words under my breath, then stopped to collect my thoughts.

After a couple minutes of thinking, I came up with a new plan. The idea was to break the cross-piece on the wooden footboard. I tried to move my legs far enough back to kick at the board but there wasn't enough slack to create enough momentum. My feet hit the board, with not nearly enough force.

My next plan of attack was to try to get to my feet and then stand on top of the bar and break it that way. That turned out to be easier said than done. My hands tied behind my back turned out to be more trouble than I had anticipated. It had a lot to do with the way they were bound as well. There was absolutely no freedom or range of motion. If he would have tied them at the wrist, then at least I might be able to use my hands to steady myself. I wriggled myself onto my side until my ankle digging into the bar prevented me from going any farther.

I remember hearing about a hiker once that had to cut his own arm off, in order to free himself from being caught under a rock. I'm not so sure that I would be able to do the same if I was presented with the same dilemma. Let's just say, that at this point I was hoping that it didn't come down to that. I was partial to having my feet, exactly where they were. I could only imagine what it would be like, to have to take such drastic measures.

Anyway, I was now lying on my side with my knees bent at 90 degrees and my one ankle digging painfully into the bar. I wriggled some more, until I was able to grab hold of the bar, or at least lay my hands over the side of it. I pushed myself up as far as my arms would allow, which wasn't nearly far enough. I spun to my left and put my right leg on top of the bar. I then realized that there was no way I'd be able to stand on top of the bar because of the way my ankles were fastened to it.

I had one option and that was to smash my shin against the bar in hopes of breaking it. I steeled myself against the pain that was coming and brought my shin down hard atop the bar. Pain exploded across my shin, and I immediately felt sick to my stomach. The bar did its part and cracked but stayed put. Without wasting any time, I brought my shin down hard on the bar again. I knew if I waited, that the pain in my leg would talk me out of doing it again.

The bar gave way from beneath my shin and sent me sprawling backward, head first into the dresser behind me. I had the briefest moment to celebrate the fact that I was free from my bed, before the back of my skull exploded from pain, when it made contact with the dresser. The mirror on the dresser fell forward, smashed and followed me to the ground. My head bounced off the floor, the room swirled and went black.

I opened my eyes. Henry and my Grandma were bent over, looking down at me. I knew that I was either dreaming or dead and based on the way I had hit my head twice in succession, I was afraid that it may be the latter. Henry reached out his hand to help me up. I was surprised to find that my hands were no longer bound together. I grabbed his and he pulled me to my feet. I grabbed at the back of my aching head with my left hand and massaged it for a few seconds. My hair was damp, and I wasn't surprised to see that my fingers were covered in blood, when I brought them in front of me.

I was getting used to these visits by Henry, but I was a little surprised to see her as well. It only served to remind me how very much I missed her.

"I'm surprised to see you both here. What's the occasion?" I asked cheerfully.

"You know very well, what the occasion is. I told you to watch out for bad Jack and look at the trouble you've gotten yourself into! I tried to warn you, over and over again," Grandma said.

"I tried Grandma. I really did, but I underestimated how devious he is I guess," I said sheepishly.

I felt like I was ten again and being scolded for letting her canary out of the cage. That was one of the few times in my life, that I remember her being truly cross with me.

"I know sweetheart. I'm sorry, I just worry that's all."

My attention switched to Henry, who was standing right beside her, looking at me with wide eyes.

"Good to see you too. I always enjoy seeing you."

He smiled widely at this, shuffling his feet a bit. His cheeks turned a little red and he looked down at his sneakers.

"I like seeing you too, Jack. I think we would have been friends, if things had worked out differently," he said quietly.

"Enough small talk! I don't mean to be rude, but we have a serious situation on our hands. We have to stop him before he hurts Vicki. You could never live with yourself, if you let that happen," Grandma said.

"I've seen too much of people hurting others. We need to stop him. I don't want anyone else hurt," Henry said.

"What do you have in mind?" I asked Grandma.

"You can start by getting up off the floor, before you bleed to death. After that, I'm sorry to say, you're on your own."

"Yeah, I don't like the looks of all that blood, Jack. I think you had better hurry," Henry said. I could hear the fear in his voice.

It took me a second to realize what they were talking about. It felt so real, so much like I was actually talking to them that I had forgotten that I was still lying on my floor in my bedroom.

Grandma reached out her hand and Henry did the same. I grabbed their hands with mine and together they repeated the same three words over and over.

"Get up. Get up! Get up!! Get up Jack!!!" they repeated in perfect unison, and by the time they were done they were yelling at me.

I opened my eyes and was disoriented at first. I was lying with my left cheek on the floor of my bedroom. Henry and Grandma were gone, and my head hurt like hell. I tried to move, but I forgot that my hands were still tied behind my back. My sore ribs did their best to remind me as well. I repositioned myself and attempted to stand up. My head swam, and I lost consciousness, slumping to the floor.

"Get up Jack!!" Grandma yelled at me.

I opened my eyes and tried to struggle to my feet, but again I lost consciousness, and fell over on my face.

"Get up Jack!!" Henry yelled.

I opened my eyes, only this time I lie there for a moment trying to get my wits about me before I tried to stand. I took a few deep breaths; in through my nose and out through my mouth. Eventually the dizzy feeling passed, and I was able to get to my feet. I bent down and stepped over my tied hands, so at least they were in front of me. I noticed the glass from the broken mirror and thought about using it to cut myself free. I figured I had better get a knife with a handle on it. I had lost enough blood already and I didn't need to be losing any more. I grabbed a knife from the wooden block holder on top of the kitchen counter. I sat on the floor and held the knife with my fingertips and sawed through the duct tape binding my ankles. Now to get my hands free. I held the knife in my mouth and started to cut the tape. I had to stop several times to prevent from gagging, but it went fairly smoothly, and I was free in a jiffy. I shook my hands a couple of times to help with the blood circulation. My hands were fine, but my fingers were all pins and needles. Once they felt normal again, I went into the bathroom and pulled a small mirror from the vanity drawer. I held it up and looked in the mirror to see the damage to my scalp. The hair was all matted and covered in blood and there was a large bump at the sight of the impact. I got a face cloth, wet it with hot water and cleaned up the area to see better. I winced with the stab of fresh pain, when the warm water touched the wound. I ignored the pain and cleaned it as best I could. I pulled the hair back to reveal a gash that was probably three inches long but surprisingly straight. I had no time for hospital waiting rooms, so I got some super glue and glued it together. It sealed the wound nicely, but the glue stuck to the skin on my fingers and some of my hair came away with them. That was certainly the least of my worries. I quickly picked the hair from my fingers and took one last peak in the mirror. Everything looked good except for the large goose egg on the back of my head. I had a splitting headache and there was no doubt that I also had a concussion. Now for my aching shin. I rolled up my pant leg to reveal my battered and bruised shin. There was a small split that ran vertically down my leg; nothing that required stitches or even glue. It was swollen purple, black and a little green thrown in for good measure. I took a couple of pain pills, quickly changed my clothes and called Hank. I glanced at the clock and it was now 8:30 p.m. I must have been unconscious for at least an hour.

I told Hank about the series of events that had transpired, and he was blown away. He was at my place within minutes.

"I called my buddy on the way over and he apologized profusely. He thought it was you. He was driving your car and he picked Vicki up. He said she acted normal, so he just assumed that it was you," Hank said, as soon as I answered the door.

"I know. I get it. That's what he was banking on. If he fooled Vicki, how was your buddy ever going to know the difference?"

"Yeah, I suppose you're right, but he still feels terrible."

"Just tell him I understand, when you see him, but for now let's get going. I have to see if I can find them."

I used the spare key and locked up quickly. We jumped into Hank's car and headed downtown. We found the car quickly enough. It was parked in front of a new, trendy Thai restaurant that had just opened. I had been wanting to go there myself, but I was hoping to take Vicki there when we got back together. Rather ironic, I thought, gritting my teeth.

I went inside, while Hank waited beside the car. A quick glance of the room and I saw that they weren't there. They had either left already or maybe they hadn't been there at all.

"Excuse me. Have you seen a young lady and a man that looked like me come in here tonight?" I asked the maître d'.

"No, sorry sir, I haven't, and I've been working since we opened for dinner."

"Okay thanks," I said and left quickly.

I went outside and motioned to Hank that I was going to try the restaurant across the street. It was a small steak house that I had never been to, because the reviews from everyone I know, were never very positive. It was however, the only other restaurant on this part of the street, so I went in to look around. I knew right away from the reaction of the maître d', that I was at the right place.

"Glad to see that you reconsidered. Will your lady friend be accompanying you this evening?" he asked, while gathering up a couple of menus.

"Um, no… Oh sorry. You think I was here earlier. No, it was my twin brother. I'm looking for him and it's kind of an emergency. So, they were here? How long ago did they leave?"

"Oh sorry, identical twins, obviously. They were here about 45 minutes ago, but they decided to go somewhere else."

"Do you happen to know where they went?"

"I wasn't eavesdropping or anything, but I did happen to hear them talking. I heard him say that he wanted to take her to a restaurant by his house. He didn't say which one, but I did happen to notice when I went out for a smoke earlier, that his car is still sitting across the road. Maybe they decided to go to the Thai restaurant across the way."

I didn't feel the need to tell him that I had been there already. I wanted to get out of there as fast as possible. Things had definitely taken a turn for the worse. I thanked him, and sprinted across the road, to where Hank was waiting for me.

"It's worse than I thought. I think he jumped with her and has taken her to his place by the sound of it."

"Why? What did you find out?" Hank asked.

"They were here earlier, but the maître d' overheard bad Jack saying that he wanted to take her to a restaurant near his place."

"Well now, that does complicate things a bit, doesn't it? We had better get over there straight away, and I think we'd better involve Bruce when we do get there. He has a good many connections with the right people, that will be able to help us," Hank said.

"I can catch up with Bruce later. For now, I just want to get to his place as quick as I can. There's no telling what he's up to."

"I know you're anxious to get there. I am too, but I need to stop to alert Bruce to what's happening. It will take a few seconds and I'm sure that he will get his people on it right away."

"Let's get going, and we can take a second to call him when we get over there, but I don't want to waste much time," I said.

"Okay, let me lock up the car and you can find a spot for us to jump, while I do."

Hank took a few seconds and by then I had located a thin spot. I went through and he followed close behind me. I didn't even notice the terrible sound of ripping cardboard and broken glass, that I had come to loathe. There were times that I didn't make the jump because I didn't want to hear that sound. This time however, I was so completely focused on finding Vicki that I never even noticed.

I was barely through the opening, before I was running, or more like limping in the direction of bad Jack's house.

"Wait a second! I have to call Bruce first," Hank called after me. "Besides I'm older than you, and shorter too. I can't keep up with you running that fast," he added.

He called him, and I could hear him answer the phone, from where I stood, ten feet away.

"Hey Hank, what's up?" he said loudly. No surprise there.

"We have a bit of a situation. I don't have time to explain the whole story, but bad Jack has Vicki and he's here somewhere. Alert your group and meet us at bad Jack's house. That's where we're going to start the search," Hank said.

"Well that is a situation, I would say. I'm on it. I'll meet you there."

That was the quickest conversation that I had ever witnessed with Bruce. He was all business, and that did a lot to reassure me.

He hung up the phone and immediately took up position beside me, as we hurried in the direction of bad Jack's house. It wasn't that far of a walk or a jog in this instance, but it felt like it took forever to get there.

We carefully approached the house. Hank went to the front door and I circled to the back. The thinking was, that he wouldn't know Hank. If they were there, he wouldn't be as alarmed as if he were to see me. All our stealth turned out to be for naught. I could tell before we got there that we were wasting our time. All but one of the lights in the house were off. There was one light in the hallway that was left on and it served to illuminate most of the house. I peered in through the window just to be sure, but I saw no movement inside. I met up with Hank at the front of the house and we moved down the street out of sight, to talk about our next plan of attack. A car pulled up, and for a second, we thought that it might be them. Hank recognized Bruce's car, so we ran out to greet him.

"Thanks for coming, but I think that you'd better pull around the corner, and we'll talk there. I don't want to be out front, if he comes home," I said.

"I would have it no other way. Let me pull around the corner as you say, and I'll introduce you, to my colleague here," Bruce said.

There was a rather official looking man riding shotgun, and he tipped his black baseball cap as he mentioned him. He was wearing black pants and a black jacket, and a stoic look on his face.

Hank and I followed them around the corner and Bruce and his colleague got out of the car. He introduced himself as Armen.

"We'll talk more later about my friend here, but for now, we have more important things to discuss, I would say," he whispered in my ear.

"Okay, well I know they were headed out to eat, but that was a while ago and they should be done by now. I figured that he might bring her back here," I said.

"That's not likely, considering he's pretending to be you. I'm thinking more in terms of a traditional date. He's trying to win her over, don't forget. Dinner and a movie, or a walk by the river, that's the kind of thing I would expect," Armen said.

I hadn't thought of it that way. I didn't know him from Adam, but I liked the way he thought and so I decided to trust him.

"Where do you think we should look?" I asked him.

"Well, in these types of situations, where the person being abducted still thinks that they are free, the perpetrator wants to keep up the illusion as long as possible, in hopes that they might actually get the abductee to comply willingly. He will continue with the façade that it's just another date. He will try to show her a good night, but if for any reason he starts to believe that things aren't going his way, that's when things could get ugly. I say that we leave one of us here to watch the house. The rest of us can spread out and check by the riverfront. Check the movie theater, the park, a comedy club, that kind of thing. We can show his picture around, and hers if you have one. I would be quick about it though. I'm not so sure that he would have jumped with her. I believe we should check your side," Armen said.

What he said made a lot of sense. That wasn't the problem. The problem was the sick feeling I got deep down in the pit of my stomach, every time I thought about him being with Vicki. The thought that she might be enjoying his company, made my skin crawl. Worse yet however, was the thought that he might tire of her and hurt her.

"You don't have a cell phone that works here, do you Jack?" Armen asked.

"No, I don't."

"Didn't think so. Okay, you go with Hank then. I'll go by myself and Bruce can stay with his car and keep an eye on the house. That way we can get in touch with one another in case one of us spots them. Sound like a plan?" Armen asked.

"Sounds like as good a plan as any, I would say," Bruce chimed in.

"Here's a picture of Vicki," I said, pulling a picture of her from my wallet.

I looked at the picture for a moment, stroking her hair with my thumb as I did. I couldn't bear it, if anything happened to her.

We split up and began our search. I felt a little nauseous as we began. All sorts of pent up negative energy was making me ill. Some of it was likely due to the loss of blood and a concussion for sure, but that was forgotten at this point. My focus was on finding her and finding her safe.

This was certainly not the way that I wanted to explain things to her. She was going to be pissed by the way that I had put her in harm's way.

Hank and I walked along the sidewalk leading to the park, in silence for the better part of five minutes.

"I'm really sorry about all of this Jack. I feel like I let you down. My guy is a real stand up guy. I'm sure he did the best he could, under the circumstances. I just question if I could have done more somehow, you know?" Hank said, breaking the silence.

"It's not your buddy's fault and it certainly isn't your fault. We have to put blame where it's deserved and that belongs solely to bad Jack. I do wish I had handled things differently from the start though. I should have told Vicki about all this a long time ago. I think now that all of this might have been avoided. It tears me up to think that I could have prevented it. I don't know what I would do if anything happened to her, you know?"

"You're being too hard on yourself. Remember, most of us don't think like him. You can call it naïve or whatever, but the fact remains that we just don't go around preparing for the worst in people."

"You're right. I know you're right. I just won't be able to relax, until Vicki is safe by my side."

"And she will be soon. You'll see," Hank said, squeezing my shoulder.

His phone rang, and my stomach clenched into a knot in nervous anticipation. He answered it quickly, but it turned out to just be Armen.

"He hasn't seen anything yet. Just checking in."

I relaxed a bit, but there was still that omni-present sick feeling, deep in the pit of my stomach, and the one thing that could help would be to find her safe.

"So, who's this Armen guy? What's his connection to the Professor, I mean Bruce?"

Old habits die hard, I guess. Especially in times of stress like these.

"That's a good question. He's a colleague of Bruce's. I'll let him explain that to you. I know he's been meaning to fill you in; he just hasn't had the chance," Hank said.

We walked in relative silence again for quite some time. We skirted the perimeter of the park, then walked through the heart of it. It was a very large and well thought out park. It was well lit along the many paths that ran throughout. There were quite a few couples enjoying the coolness of the late summer's evening. Some were sitting on park benches, or on the edges of one of the fountains or strolling hand in hand down one of the paths. There was no sign of bad Jack or Vicki, however.

"I have to sit for a couple of minutes. My damn knee is killing me," Hank said, as he sat on the closest park bench and produced a couple of pain pills from his pocket. He swallowed them dry and sat rubbing his knee.

I sat as patiently as I could, waiting for him to recover a bit. I was sure he wouldn't be long. He knew how antsy I was to keep moving.

I had a minute to reflect on all that happened in the last few weeks, leading up to this point. It's funny how your mind copes with moments of stress, such as these. I had been seeing Henry in my dreams and now Grandma showed up today. It was nice seeing her. I miss her quite a bit, when I allow myself to think of her. I allowed myself to be pulled away from the stress of the moment, if only briefly.

Grandma had snuck out of the retirement home and gotten a taxi into town. She came to the school, signed me out and we kind of played hooky together. It wasn't the first time that she had done it and like many things that she and I shared, it was our little secret. We didn't have the typical Grandma and grandson relationship, obviously. It went deeper than just the secrets that we shared. She was more of a confidant and friend than she was a Grandma. I never viewed her as an old lady. I always valued her advice and the time that we spent together. I don't mean to sound like a broken record, but I really do miss her a lot. Most people have that one relative in their life that means the world to them and for me that was my Grandma. I look at my life in terms of two segments. Well, actually that has changed a bit now. I was going to say that I look at my life in terms of my life before she died and then my life afterwards. That has changed somewhat now. I now include the time before I met Vicki and after I met her into the mix.

Anyway, it was a day in early October. The weather was perfect. The sun was shining, and it wasn't too warm or too cool. She came to the school and got me out of class without warning. I was surprised to see her and at first, I was concerned that something was wrong. Those fears fell by the way side, as soon as I saw her. It was hard to tell at that moment, that she was the adult and I was the child. She was smiling, and I saw the nervous anticipation written all over her face. She hurriedly ushered me outside the school, where we could be alone. She then told me in a hushed voice, as though it was a life or death secret, what her plans for the day were.

Every year during the first week of October the fair comes to our small town. She said that it had changed a lot over the years, of course, but that she still enjoyed it and looked forward to it every year. It was still morning and none of the rides opened until 11a.m. but that gave us time to see the animal building. There were chickens, ducks, rabbits, pigeons and geese in the one building. In another building, there were cows, pigs, sheep, goats and a llama. We fed the animals and petted the ones that would let us. Then we moved on to the produce building that showcased vegetables, fruits and gourds from the local farmers. We made it about half - way through the last building that had art work from the neighbouring schools in it, before I got bored and wanted to leave. Grandma took me outside and we got a corn dog smothered in mustard. I gulped it down and she bought me a second one, no questions asked. The corn dog was delicious, and the animals were okay, but the real reason we were there was for the rides.

She was like a little kid, giddy with excitement. I think back on that day, and about how so many of us forget to laugh and have fun as we get older. That's a trap that I have certainly fallen into these past few weeks.

We rode, ride after ride for the better part of four hours. Both of us agreed, that the Zipper was the best ride of all. It was like an elongated Ferris wheel that had about twenty cages on it. Each cage held as many as three people and they rocked front to back and would even roll completely over if the momentum was right. They loaded the ride from the bottom and then moved the cages upwards until they were full. From the top of the ride we could see the entire fair, it was that high. Grandma rocked the cage back and forth and I screamed in fear at first, but eventually I came to love it. Once the ride started, it flung us up and over the top of the ride and then we were sent hurtling back toward the earth. It was a different ride every time, depending on how the momentum caught the cages. Sometimes we went rushing straight at the ground and it felt as though we might hit, and other times we spun wildly over and over again. It is still my favourite ride to this very day. We rode the Zipper more times than I could count, and many countless times since.

She took me back to the school and dropped me off, just in time for the bell to ring signalling the end of the day.

"How was your day?" Helen asked.

"Not too bad," I said, turning my head to hide my enormous smile. "Not too bad at all."

The time it took to remember those events, took mere seconds, but already I was growing impatient. I wanted to be going again. I was about to urge Hank to press on, but he beat me too it.

"I don't want to hold you up any longer. Let's go. The pain pills should kick in soon enough," he said, rubbing his sore knee once more for good measure, before standing up.

Without saying a word, I popped up from the bench and started walking down the path. Hank, to his credit kept up.

We had now covered about as much of the park as we could. When we got out onto the street, he checked in with Armen to tell him, that so far, our search had come empty. Armen hadn't had any luck either and Bruce reported no movement on the home front.

We set off toward the waterfront in hopes of finding them there. The waterfront was much the same as the park. There were couples walking hand in hand on the path by the river and sitting on park benches overlooking the water. Normally, I would get a warm feeling, seeing all these couples enjoying the weather and each other's company. Not today however. I cringed at the thought of bad Jack and Vicki walking hand in hand along one of these paths, like all these couples in love.

It was a good mile of waterfront to explore, and all along the length of it were little shops, boutiques, restaurants and bars. I checked in every window as we passed by. I knew that if there was a patio open or if she were inside, she would want to be sitting where she could see the river. She wasn't big into shopping for nothing, so I ruled out the shops and boutiques.

The walk down the waterfront took half an hour or so and produced nothing. Hank checked in with Armen and Bruce and they also hadn't seen them. I was beginning to believe that maybe they weren't on this side after all.

We decided to all meet back at bad Jack's house. Not because we thought that he'd turn up there, but because Bruce was there with his car and that would make getting around that much easier. It made sense that he wouldn't come back here with her anyway, we were just covering all the bases. Now we weren't entirely sure where to go from here, but sometimes luck just happens to be on your side.

While we were discussing our next plan of attack, guess who decided to join the party?

"Jack, what's up man? Good to see ya! I was hoping to run into you. Listen! I've been trying to catch up to the other Jack for the better part of two days now. He's been busy that's for sure. I've been biding my time, hoping to get the element of surprise. Normally I wouldn't be too concerned by him as you're well aware of, but I saw him buying a hand gun from some dude in a back alley yesterday. It just became a completely different scenario. You know what I mean?" George said.

"I know exactly what you mean," I said and recounted the events of earlier in the day.

"That's fucked up. I assume you're looking for him then?"

"Yeah, and he has Vicki with him."

"Well, now that's even more fucked up!" George said.

"Let me introduce you to the rest of the team."

When the introductions had concluded, we tried to come up with a new plan.

"Like I said before, I've been watching him, and earlier today I saw him jump, or slide or whatever you people do, but I haven't seen him return and I haven't seen her either," George said.

"So, I've led us on a wild goose chase then," I said, turning to the others.

"At least we know where they aren't, and that's one step in the right direction, I would say," Bruce said.

"Let's get down to business. It appears, we need to go over to the other side in order to finish our business. Can we trust this guy?" Armen asked, pointing towards George.

He was visibly disturbed by having his integrity questioned, and probably a little disturbed by being talked about as though he weren't even there.

"Absolutely. I would trust him with my life," I said, looking at George.

We shared a bit of a chuckle at that.

Armen continued without acknowledging.

"I've entrusted Bruce to fill you in at his leisure, but for now, let me tell you simply that I am the director of The Alliance on this side. I'm not here because I'm so interested In Jack Armstrong and his girlfriend Vicki. I'm here to make sure that the other Jack is kept under control and dealt with, permanently if need be," Armen said.

He turned to George and continued.

"I'm going to give you the ability to jump to our sister world, for the time being. I think that you will be an asset to us, in our mission there," he said.

Armen produced a large, gaudy, gold rope style necklace from an inside pocket of his jacket. It had a flat, oval amulet attached to the end of it. The turquoise surface appeared to be alive. It turned and swirled with wisps of white that looked like clouds moving and changing across its surface.

George held out his hand, without taking his eyes off the amulet. Armen placed it in his hand, and George continued to stare at it. His mouth was slightly open, a little spittle escaped and ran down the side of his mouth. His eyes were wide and vacant. He stood that way for a couple of seconds, until Armen began to speak again. This seemed to break him free from the trance that he was in, and he looked up slowly, dreamily.

"Don't worry. Everyone has the same initial reaction. Those of us, lucky enough to be born with the ability to jump between the worlds acquire our power slowly over years. You have been given that all at once. A little disconcerting at first, but it will pass. All you have to do, is find a thin spot, rip it open and walk through. That should prove easy enough, since you can watch us do it and then follow us. Are you okay with that?" he asked.

"Follow... Yes... Okay," George said dreamily.

CHAPTER SIXTEEN

Bruce went through first and then Hank, followed by me, George and finally Armen. We all gathered in a circle like a football huddle calling a play. The thing was, that none of us had our next play. God only knew where they could be.

"I'm going to call The Alliance on this side, to keep them apprised of the situation and see if they can help. They will dispatch someone from our side though, given the circumstances. In the old days, this would be easy. All citizens capable of jumping between the worlds were closely monitored and had tracking devices implanted, but the human rights movements of the '60's put an end to that. Now we have to identify individuals that are a threat and monitor them manually. Your bad Jack definitely made that list, so they may know where he is," Armen said.

He made his call, and after several minutes on hold, he got to talk to someone. I couldn't hear what was being said, but I could tell from his body language, that at least it wasn't bad news.

He came back to the huddle and repeated what he was told on the phone.

"Okay, so it looks like they were monitoring him earlier in the day. He spent several hours at a residence on the east side."

"Yeah, that was my place! Good job, thanks guys!" I said, interrupting him. "Sorry, continue," I said.

"No problem. Anyway, he has been in the downtown core all evening, but now it seems as though he is in a car heading west."

"Do you know where they may be heading, that would be west of the downtown core?" Armen asked.

"Vicki's place is west of here. Maybe they are going there," I said.

"That's as good a bet as any, I would say," Bruce said.

"My car isn't too far from here. Come on!" Hank said.

"Don't forget he is armed," George said.

"I've got it covered," Armen said, patting his jacket. "I'm going to call for back up as well. What's the address?" he asked.

"205 Shellard lane, apartment 2a," I answered.

Vicki had moved there shortly after we had started dating. It was in a nice section of town and the rent was surprisingly affordable. I helped her move on the most miserable, rainy day of the entire year. We spent as much time trying to dry things off afterwards, as we did moving in the first place. Her brother John helped for some of it, but we did most of it ourselves. I would have been content to just have everything moved and deal with putting things away later. Vicki however, had to have everything in its place that night, before we went to bed. I ended up falling asleep on the sofa, mid-sentence, I think. She woke me up several hours later and escorted me to the bedroom wearing a little black nightie that surely wasn't meant to keep her warm at night, I can tell you that much. That was my job I guess, and one that I was all too happy to help with.

We spent many nights there in the beginning, but as time went by, we spent about half the time at my place as well. Before all this mess with bad Jack, I had started to think that we were ready for us to get a place to call our own. I had been wanting to buy a ring and ask her to marry me, but things had gone south in our relationship recently, as you well know.

We got to Vicki's place and sure enough there were lights on. There were cars parked everywhere in front of the building. Cars parked up and down both sides of the street, and the thump, thump, thump of music playing, was coming from somewhere inside.

Her building was ordinarily a quiet one, but recently two of the apartments had been rented to some college kids, and there goes the neighbourhood, as they say.

I wanted to go running in there to save her. That was my initial response anyway, but that would be a foolish thing to do, and I knew it. In case I wasn't sure though, Armen laid out for me how things were going to go down.

"I know you want to see Vicki, but he's armed, and you aren't. I've called for backup but I'm not anticipating too much trouble. I'll go in first, with Bruce here at my side. You and Hank stay back, and I'll let you know when the coast is clear. George, you can stay here on street level, in case they aren't at Vicki's and they show up while we are up there. Okay?" Armen said.

"Don't worry Jack, everything will be just fine. A couple more minutes, and this nightmare will be over, for good."

"Thanks Bruce. Thanks for everything," I said.

"My pleasure my boy. Gives an old coot like me something to do, besides sit in my study and read," he said, squeezing my hand.

We crept carefully in the front door and up the stairs. Armen and Bruce were in the lead. They had their guns in hand but tucked into their coat pockets, in case there were some party-goers roaming the halls. We walked slowly down the hall and stopped just short of Vicki's door.

"Okay, you stay here. I'm going to knock on the door and hope that she answers," Armen said.

Armen knocked loudly on her door and then waited, with his gun held in front of him. He stood that way for a minute, but no one came to the door. He knocked loudly again and waited. I saw him tense and he muttered something to Bruce beside him. I could tell from their reactions that they heard someone stirring inside. Bruce peeked over his shoulder and winked at me, a small devilish grin appearing at the corners of his mouth. He was clearly enjoying the excitement. I on the other hand, just wanted it to be over quickly and safely.

From my vantage point I couldn't see her door. I was probably twenty feet down the hall and couldn't hear any noise coming from her apartment, nor could I hear what Armen had said to Bruce. My focus was on the spot in front of them, to see who answered the door.

After what seemed like an eternity, I heard the tell-tale sound of the dead bolt being slid back out of place. She had been bugging me to oil it so that it would slide easier, but I kept putting it off.

I couldn't see the door open, but I knew that it had, because Armen sprang into action and Bruce wasn't far behind. Armen lowered his gun, reached out quickly with his left hand and pulled Vicki out into the hall and Bruce slammed the door behind her. She was bewildered, scared and I never saw her look more beautiful. What a sight for sore eyes. There she was, safely away from bad Jack, without incident. I exhaled deeply, and a great feeling of relief came over me. I took a step toward her, and was about to call out to her, when...

"Well hello Jacky boy. What brings you by?" bad Jack said, from behind me.

I spun to face him. He lifted his gun and pointed it at me and stopped in his tracks, assessing the situation. He cocked his head to the side so that he could see past me and down the hall. He knelt, placing the bag of ice that he was carrying on the hallway carpet, then stood back up. He placed his other hand on his gun and continued to point it at me.

"I told you to stay put, until I came back for you. You don't follow instructions very well, do you? Now look what you've done. You've gone and upset the love of our lives," he said mockingly.

I turned my head to look in Vicki's direction. She was standing in between Armen and Bruce with her mouth open, her eyes wide as saucers. Bruce and Armen held her with one hand and pointed their guns down the hall in my direction, with the other. Hank did his best to just stay out of the way, somewhere in between.

I turned back to face him. He was smiling his twisted smile, that I had come to loathe.

"Come over here. I want to tell you a little secret," he said smugly.

"Stay where you are Jack! I'm coming to you," I heard Armen say, from behind me.

"Easy. Stay put, or he's dead, and I'll take my chances where I'm concerned," bad Jack said to Armen.

"Now come over here Jack," bad Jack said.

"It's okay. Just keep Vicki safe, I'll be fine," I said, and walked toward him.

When I got close enough, he grabbed me, spun me around and put his gun to my temple. I was now looking down the hall toward her. Vicki was still standing in the same spot and her eyes remained wide, staring vacantly down the hall in my direction. Armen had halted his advance a couple of steps in front of her. Bruce was still standing beside her and holding on to her arm.

"I guess I should have killed you when I had the chance. It's just that, I like to play with my quarry a bit. It'll be the death of me someday, but I just can't help myself. I'm just too damn playful for my own good," bad Jack, whispered in my ear.

"It's about time you showed up. I was beginning to wonder if you were going to make it," Armen said.

I was confused. I thought that maybe he was trying to fake bad Jack out, that maybe he was trying to get him to turn his head, so that he could get a shot. The sound of footsteps echoed from behind me and the smell of perfume filled the hallway. I turned to see who it was and couldn't believe my eyes, or my misfortune.

Bad Jack, turned to see who was there as well, but kept the gun pressed firmly against my temple.

"Hey Dad, what's up?" he said cheerfully.

Bad Jack's Dad and Victoria were standing there. Karl lifted a gun and pointed it in my direction. I was surprised to see Victoria there, since she told me that day at his office building, that they weren't an item. She seemed like a pleasant girl when I had talked to her, and I couldn't believe that she was involved with him. I was even more surprised now by the turn of events that had befallen me.

"Good to see you Dad. I wasn't sure how I was going to get out of this pickle. What are you doing here Vicki? Oooh I get it. A little side action, hey Pops? Good for you, not bad, not bad," Jack said.

"You shouldn't have gotten messed up in all of this," Karl said.

"You tell him Dad!" bad Jack said.

"I can't allow you to continue to interfere with the lives of these people," he said.

"Yeah!" bad Jack said, and spun my body around to join my head, facing down the hall towards Karl. "Let's get out of here!" he said, pressing the muzzle of the gun hard into my temple again.

He shuffled forward, dragging me with him.

"Stay where you are Jack!"

"Come on Daddy! Aren't you happy to see your little boy? I know I haven't been visiting as much as I should, but I would say that's more on you. Anyway, let's clean up this mess and go grab a drink or something. What do you say? What the Hell, we can bring the girls along with us," he said, nodding in Victoria's direction.

"Shut up Jack!"

"Dad...Daddy...Is that anyway to talk to your baby boy?" he said, throwing his head back and laughing.

He snapped his head forward, when he realized that his concentration had been broken.

"Nice try! Daddy didn't raise no fool," he said, to Karl.

"How do you see this ending Jacky boy? I know I'm not Dad's favourite person at the moment, but I'm blood after all. Time to make our move and get out of here," he whispered in my ear.

He took another step toward Karl.

"I hate to do this. I'm sorry but I don't have a choice," Karl said.

"See, I told you so, Jacky boy. No real decision after all," bad Jack whispered again, his tongue licking at the inside of my ear.

Karl's gun roared in his hand and I closed my eyes, waiting for the pain. I looked through my fingers at the floor, waiting for my blood to start spilling onto the carpet beneath my feet. I knew that when people go into shock that they sometimes can't feel the pain right away, but I expected to feel some type of sensation. I peeled my fingers from in front of my eyes, to reveal bad Jack, lying in a pool of blood at my feet. His eyes were open, and his mouth was closed in a tight thin smile. His gun was lying off to one side. His twisted grin would never again mock me, except for in my dreams.

My initial thought was that Karl had missed, and that it was my turn next. He lowered his gun and put it away. He stood for a moment looking down at his dead son. He gathered himself, stepped over his lifeless body and picked up the gun. He clapped me on the shoulder as he brushed past me and walked to the end of the hall to meet Armen. He shook hands with Armen and they whispered back and forth a couple of times. He shook hands with Bruce and then walked back towards me. Karl knelt beside him and checked for a pulse. He shook his head and stayed that way for several minutes holding his wrist. He sighed heavily and then stood up.

Vicki was still standing where she had been the entire time. She had covered her mouth with her hands, and tears were running down her face. Victoria spoke from behind me, startling me.

"Good to see you again, Jack. I wish it were under better circumstances, but at least Vicki is safe," she said.

I nodded in agreement. "So, you're part of the Alliance?" I asked.

"Yes, Karl's partner."

"Now it makes sense," I said, turning to walk toward Vicki.

I was apprehensive as to how she would receive me, but I just wanted to hold her in my arms and comfort her.

She saw me walking toward her and she pulled free from Bruce, who was still holding her by the arm. I gathered her in my arms and held her tightly.

"I can't believe this is happening. I can't believe it. It's like a bad dream," she said. "I thought he was you at first! Who was he? I didn't know you had a twin! What the hell is going on?"

I didn't say a word. I just held her tighter. After all this time, and all that had happened; I just wanted to feel the warmth of her body next to mine. It was like coming home after a long trip, and feeling that comfortable, safe feeling, that only home can provide.

"I'll explain as best as I can..."

"And who are these guys? she asked, cutting me off.

"I'll explain everything. Let's go inside."

"Take them inside and I'll clean up this mess," Karl said to Armen, as he stood looking at his son, lying in the middle of the hallway. He stood shaking his head for a minute. As we turned to go into Vicki's apartment, I saw a couple other gentlemen in black suits, come up the stairs and stop where Karl was standing.

"I'll go downstairs and get George," Hank said, walked down the hall and out of sight.

The rest of us filed into her apartment and sat in her living room. Minutes later, Hank returned with George and they let themselves in as well.

Vicki's apartment was a decent size, but it felt small with all these people in it.

"I'm sure you have a lot of questions, under the circumstances, I don't blame you. I think that Jack can answer the important ones tonight. We'll leave you two alone. We'll get in touch with you in the morning and go over the rest, if you're up to it. Maybe it's best if we meet in Bruce's study hall, there'll be more room there. Either way, we will have to have a briefing, and your attendance will be mandatory. I'll thank you in advance for your cooperation and have a good night," Armen said.

"Jack, I need to talk to you, off the record as well," Karl said.

"Tomorrow. Leave it be, until tomorrow," Armen said.

Armen got up and made his way to the door. Reluctantly Karl got up and followed him. Hank, George and Victoria were the next to get up, and then Bruce.

He walked over, shook my hand and then placed his hand on Vicki's.

"Things will get better now, I would say," he said to me, and then turned to Vicki.

"I know I'm a stranger to you my dear, but I feel like I know you from the conversations that Jack and I have had. I know that you both have been through a lot, but you have each other, and that is truly the most important thing. Good night my dear. Good night my boy. I'll see you tomorrow," Bruce said, and then joined the others at the door.

There we were just the two of us. The apartment felt impossibly large now, except for the elephant in the room.

"I don't want to stay here tonight. Can we go to your house and can you drive? I shouldn't be driving. It'll give me time to think. I have a lot of questions I need to sort through."

"Sure," I said.

Vicki was back in my life, just like that. All the anguish from the last few weeks was still there in the background. The fear still remained, that she may not understand or forgive me right away, but for now, it felt great that I was sitting here, with the love of my life.

"Okay. Do you need to pack anything?"

"No. Let's just go," she said, tiredly.

We went out into the hall. I held her close and shielded her eyes from the large blood spot, that filled the middle of the hallway. Remarkably however, there was no sign of blood or bad Jack for that matter. There was no sign that anything had happened here at all. I removed my hand from over Vicki's eyes and she looked down the hall, hesitantly. She looked up at me questioningly, and I just answered by shrugging my shoulders, and continued. I wanted to get out of this place, as much as she did.

We got in her car and navigated around all the cars that were parked by her building. The steady thump, thump, thump of music still filled the night. A short, silent car ride later and we were at my place. I let us in and ushered her into the living room.

"I have to clean up a mess from earlier, first," I said.

I swept up the broken mirror and then mopped the blood from the floor. I was amazed to see just how much blood there was. No wonder I didn't feel quite right earlier.

"I'm sorry about that. I had a little spill earlier and I thought that you had seen quite enough blood for one evening."

"Uh-huh," she said.

"Are you ready to talk or do you need to wait?" I asked.

"I want to wait, but I'll never be able to sleep, until I find out what the Hell just happened."

"Let me start by saying I'm so sorry that you had to go through all of this. I wanted to tell you so many times, but this was a secret that my Grandma and I shared. You know how close we were, and it felt like I was betraying her by telling our secret. I had finally decided to tell you, but then things started going wrong and you wanted your space. Then I was caught between telling you and giving you your space that you needed. I figured that if I pushed, then it might just push you further away."

"So, when things were going wrong, as you say. That was the other guy, the one that looked like you?" she asked.

"Yes. That's why I didn't know what you were talking about, when you accused me of acting strangely."

"I see. So, what's this secret, that you shared, and how does he fit in? Is he your twin brother or something?"

"This is going to be hard for you to believe. It might take a while. Do you want something to drink before I continue?"

"Sure, I'll take a couple of pain pills and a glass of wine. I have a smashing headache. Then I want to hear everything!"

I got her the pills and wine like she asked, then began my story. I started with what happened at the nursing home when I was a child. I told her the stories that Grandma told me, about when she was young, and she first found out from her Father about the other world. I told her about bad Jack and how Grandma switched us at birth. I left the part out, about him being a serial rapist and overall bad guy. She sat for long periods of time without asking a question. Hell, she barely blinked. When I did pause, the questions flowed from her in waves. I did my very best to answer all her questions, and for the most part, I think I handled them well enough. I told her that I still had a lot of unanswered questions myself, that would hopefully be answered when we sat down with Bruce and his friends tomorrow. I did get around to telling her how I was tied up twice in one week, once by bad Jack and once by George, but that George and I were now friends.

I talked for an hour and she listened intently. She had many questions, but I was amazed by how well she was taking all of this. I was also amazed that she wasn't in the least bit mad at me, like I thought that she would be. She was very understanding of what I went through as well.

When I was finished telling my story, I went into the kitchen to get a drink to douse the flames in the back of my throat, from all the talking. I came back into the living room and sat on the sofa beside her.

"Any more questions?"

"This is all incredible stuff. I only have one more question for right now. More of a statement really. I want you to show me the other world. We can explore more tomorrow, but for now I would be happy with a glimpse," she said, smiling, her eyes twinkling.

"Okay, let's go then," I said, grabbing her by the hand and leading her out into the back yard.

I stood facing the back of the property looking for a thin spot. There weren't usually any thin spots here, so I wasn't surprised to not find one. Thin spots weren't always in the same spots, but quite often they were close by.

"We'll have to try somewhere else. There aren't any thin spots here," I said.

We went back through the house and out the front. The side yard between the houses, offered what we were searching for.

"Do you want to jump, or just look for now?" I asked.

"I don't know. Does it hurt?" she asked.

"Only if you fall," I said laughing. "It's just like walking through a door."

"Well in that case, of course I want to go," she said.

I located a thin spot and prepared Vicki for what she was about to see and hear. She thought that it sounded cool when I ripped a hole between the worlds. That was something that we were going to have to agree to disagree on. She came with me through the hole without any reservations whatsoever. All the unhappiness and trauma of the last few weeks was forgotten, and we were like two little kids on Christmas morning. Vicki, more than me of course, was having the time of her life. I wouldn`t say that it ever got boring for me, but it certainly didn`t have the same wow factor that it once did. The wow factor for her on the other hand, was at an all-time high.

"This is so incredible. I wish you would have shared this with me before."

"I know, I'm sorry. I wish that I did as well."

"No. I understand why you didn't. I mean I can't believe that I've been missing out on this. I can't believe that this has been kept from the masses, without someone finding out."

"I guess they have their ways of keeping it quiet," I said, shuddering to think what their methods might be.

Vicki and I walked hand in hand in the park for a while. I thought about the couples I had seen earlier. I was glad for the chance to experience this with her.

"We can come here whenever you like, but what do you say we head back. It's been a long day, and to be honest, I'm not feeling all that well."

"Sure, as long as you promise to bring me here again," she said.

"Of course, I will. I promise; any time you want," I said, laughing. "Come on let's go home."

CHAPTER SEVENTEEN

We were both exhausted when we got back to my house and went straight to bed. It felt so amazing to be in Vicki's arms. I never wanted to be apart from her ever again.

I awoke once during the night. I saw bad Jack standing in the dark room, his twisted grin visible in the moonlight for a second and then he was gone. Neither Grandma nor Henry came calling on this night. They must have known that I needed my rest, and they left me alone.

When I woke up the next morning, I had to check beside me to make sure I hadn't dreamt it all. Vicki turned to face me and smiled.

"I missed you," she said.

"I missed you too. I love you."

"I love you too," she said, kissed me and put her arms around me. "Let's get moving. I want to go back over and explore a bit, before we have to meet up with your friend and his associates. I'm curious as to what they have to say."

I took the time to brush my teeth and eat while she tugged at my arm, trying to hurry me up. She was so anxious to get moving, that she couldn't stop fidgeting.

"Are you going to be all day. I would like to go before the day is gone," she said, with her hands on her hips.

"Okay, okay. Let's go," I said, laughing.

We made the jump and we explored for nearly four hours. We walked through the park, by the waterfront and downtown. She was smiling the entire time. It was so great to see her enjoying herself. I went into more detail about the things that Grandma had taught me. I had a lifetime of lessons and information regarding this place. It was impossible to teach her all of it in one morning, even though she was about the most enthusiastic student that any teacher could ask for. She asked questions in such rapid succession, that my head was spinning from them all. This place seemed just that little bit more special, being able to share it with her.

"So, you like this place then?"

"It's awesome. It has more green spaces than home. I think it's more the idea of being here, than it is the actual place itself. I just can't believe that this is happening!" she said, excitedly.

I squeezed her hand, kissed her and laughed at her infectious enthusiasm.

"What do you say we go see the others? I'm interested to see what they have to say. There are some questions that I hope they can answer for me as well," I said.

We showed up at Bruce's study hall before anyone else got there. He answered the door and led us into his study.

"Good to see you again my dear. I can tell from the smile on your face, that things are better today then when we last met."

"Absolutely. This is incredible!" she said.

"You look better today as well, my boy."

"I know you have a lot of questions, so let's get to it shall we. Armen won't be here, he's off on official business, but I think I can fill in all the blanks in his absence. Karl will be here later, but by then, I should have wrapped up what I want to tell you. If you have any questions as we go along, please don't hesitate to interrupt me. I tend to ramble a bit once I get going," he said, brushing his hair back with the palms of his hands.

The hair immediately started to stand up again, and Vicki squeezed my hand. I could tell that she was trying to stifle a laugh.

"Okay, we're all yours, enlighten us," I said.

"I'll try my best. Let me start by saying, that I can't even imagine the emotions that the two of you must be experiencing. I do know however, that you will be able to get through anything, as long as you have each other. Anyway, enough of an old fool's sentimental thoughts.

I know Armen can be a little intimidating at times, but he means well. This meeting would normally be an official meeting, held at the Alliance headquarters downtown, but given the circumstances, we decided to forgo the normal protocol. Besides we're friends, no need for formality here.

"Should we be worried?" I asked, laughing nervously.

"Of course not. I just want to fill in the blanks for you that's all. There is a standard non-disclosure agreement, that you must sign before we're done here, that's all. So, you're probably wondering what the Alliance is. The Alliance was started back in the 1920's. It was originally founded by a group of friends that could jump between the worlds. It started as a club of sorts. It was just a bunch of friends getting together to tell stories and share experiences that they had while travelling between the worlds. As the members' numbers increased, things changed. Rules were introduced to preserve the group's secrecy and eventually they had to adopt rules, to deal with those that would try to abuse their ability to jump and to use it for criminal activity. That set up an entire new branch of the Alliance, which sadly enough takes up most of our resources at the present. With every organization, there has to be heads of each department. Armen is a kind of watch dog. He oversees everything, and delegates responsibility to the proper branches. Karl oversees enforcement and Victoria is his second in command. I'm in charge of contacting people that are new to the jumping game. I have the best job of them all, I would say. I get to see the excitement and the wonderment on all those new faces," he said, as he turned to look directly at Vicki. "See!" he said.

She was of course still smiling, and she smiled even more, when Bruce addressed her.

"I'll continue. The Alliance started on this side, but shortly thereafter it expanded to your side as well. Today there are branches on both sides, and we are constantly working together to ensure our anonymity and the safety of all citizens in both towns."

"So, this only happens in these two towns then?" Vicki asked.

"Yes. Curiously this phenomenon only happens in these two towns. There doesn't seem to be any thin spots anywhere else; none that we have found yet anyway, and there have been extensive searches done," he said.

"So, how is it that the masses have never found out about all of this?" she asked.

"A lot of resources and time have been devoted to keeping all of this quiet. We aren't talking about a significant percentage of the population here. There are roughly fifteen thousand people in each town and roughly one in seven hundred people have the ability to jump. On top of that, it seems to be limited to very few families, so it isn't as widespread as you may think. Occasionally something does go wrong and they are dealt with on a case by case basis," Bruce said.

"But you didn't really answer the question?" she said, smiling one of her little sarcastic smiles.

"I did answer the question my dear. Sometimes the answers we seek, serve only to generate more questions. Let me just say, that if you ever have a secret you want to tell, well, it's safe with me," he said and laughed

Vicki and I laughed at that and Bruce went on to tell more stories that had us laughing again and again. He answered as many questions as he could, and she had lots of them. The one question that I had however, would have to wait.

"Bruce, I was wondering about Karl. I know that you said he was in charge of enforcement, along with Victoria, but his own son. I can't believe that he could go through with it. I can't even imagine," I said.

"I know. I feel for him. I really do, but he has a job to do. There's more to the story but I'll let him tell you, when he gets here. You know first-hand what bad Jack was like. He was bad through and through. No one knew that more than his Dad, believe me," he said sadly, shaking his head slowly.

"All his scrapes with the law were hard for him to take, but the rape charges were an unbearable burden for him. Anyway, I've said too much like usual. I should let him say what he wants to say on the subject, when he gets here. Shouldn't be too much longer."

Vicki was visibly shaken by the mention of rape charges. I squeezed her hand and for the moment she let it be.

"I have a question. It's a little off topic but here goes. Did my Grandma know about the Alliance? She left me an awful lot of information, but nowhere did it ever mention the Alliance," I asked.

"Yes, she did, is the short answer. There's a longer one, but I'll let Karl tell you. The Alliance would not have taken too kindly to her leaving information about them in the folder that she left for you. To be honest, she shouldn't have made the folder in the first place and I should have stopped her, but...well, you know. She'd have gotten herself into a spot of trouble, I would say, if the Alliance found out."

"Now, I have a couple more questions. One. What makes you think I want to talk to bad Jack's Dad anyway? Two. Why do you talk about the Alliance as if you aren't a part of it?" I asked.

"I can understand your reservations where Karl is concerned, but he is nothing like him. I can assure you of that. Secondly. Yes, it is true that I belong to the Alliance, but I have a very different roll within the organization. Perhaps I didn't make myself clear, when I spoke about it earlier. I enjoy meeting new people. I enjoy teaching people about jumping between the worlds. I don't get too caught up in the day to day grind of the administration of the Alliance. I'm more of a free spirit. I march to my own drum, if you will, and for the most part they don't interfere with my affairs. Does that make sense?" Bruce asked.

"It makes perfect sense," I said.

"Good. Now, I think we need to have a few drinks to lighten the mood. Beer okay?" he asked. "Vicki, beer okay?"

We both nodded in agreement and he went to fetch us a couple of beers.

"I'm expecting my brothers later, after Karl leaves that is. You should stay, it'll be fun," he said, handing us our beers.

We drank a few beers each while Bruce entertained us with one story after another. I could tell that Vicki felt the same way that I had, when I first met him. He made you feel so comfortable from the very start, like you had known him for a long time. His brothers were much the same way.

"Wait until you meet his brothers! You're going to love them!" I said.

"If they are anything like Bruce, I'm sure you're right," she said.

"Aww you're too kind," Bruce said, blushing a little.

He looked at his watch, and almost as if on cue, there was a knock at the door. The sound echoed through the large hall and into his study.

"That's probably Karl," Bruce said, jumping up to answer the door. "Be back in a jiffy."

We could hear Bruce's voice like he was standing next to us. Vicki covered her mouth to stifle a laugh.

"He's quite the character. I love him. Can we keep him? His hair is awesome too," she said, laughing.

"Wait 'til you meet his brothers."

"Why, what's up with them?"

"You'll see. I don't want to ruin the surprise."

He came back, and sure enough, it was Karl that was at the door.

"I'm going to make a beer run. I'll leave you three to talk for a while. If I'm not here, then there's no chance of me monopolizing the conversation," he said, and was gone.

"I guess there's no need to introduce myself, but I will anyway. My name is Karl Armstrong," he said, extending his hand to Vicki and then to me.

We shook his hand, and he continued.

"I'd like to get the official Alliance business out of the way, then we can talk, and I can answer any questions that you may have," he said, producing two pieces of paper, two pens from his inside coat pocket, and placed one in front of each of us.

"Read them over and sign at the bottom, please. If you have any questions, I'll be happy to answer them."

"I have one. What if we don't want to sign them?" Vicki said.

Karl took the pen from in front of her and put it back in his pocket.

"I think you'll find, that once you have read them, that we aren't asking that much," he said patiently.

"We'll see," she said and began to read hers.

It was a standard non-disclosure agreement. We would be agreeing not to tell, show or otherwise inform anyone about the events of last night, nor were we to make the presence known of the sister world, jumping or the

Alliance, by any method, not limited to the internet, recording, media storage devices, written or verbally. It went on, but that was the gist of it.

"What happens if we do tell?" she said.

It was just like her to test the boundaries of authority. I for one had no problem signing it. I don't think she did either, deep down, but she just wanted to make sure that her civil liberties weren't being compromised.

"Let me say this. I'm sure that you can appreciate, why this needs to be something of a secret. This is not something that we are willing to have the masses aware of. It might cause chaos on a scale that we wouldn't have the resources to control. So, to get to your question. We would do what is necessary to control and remove the threat if need be. You can read between the lines. Let's just say, that it's in your best interest; hell, it's in all our best interests, for you to keep this quiet," he said.

"You still didn't answer my question, but whatever, I'll sign," Vicki said.

I had already signed mine and slid it back across the table towards him. She placed her signed copy on top of mine.

"Okay, so that's out of the way. Now I want to talk to you on a more personal level."

He took a couple of deep breaths and then tried to speak but nothing came out. His eyes welled up with tears and he wiped at his eyes. He got up and walked to the refrigerator to grab a beer for himself and one for each of us. Vicki and I exchanged glances, accepted our beers and settled in to listen to what Karl had to say.

"My son was a troubled man, but I would have to be one cold son of a bitch to not be conflicted by the events that led to the incident last night. I tried to be the best Father that I could possibly be, but he was always a little off, you know? From the time he was small, I sensed in him something, that wasn't quite right. It's the old age argument, of nature versus nurture. There was nothing in his upbringing that should have made him the way he was. He was never abused or neglected, and neither his Mom nor I were alcoholics or workaholics. We tried to provide a good home for him, and I think we did, for most of his childhood. Lately his Mother has been having a hard time dealing with his indiscretions, shall we say, and that has led to some of her own demons surfacing. But, that's another story. You're probably wondering why I'm telling you all of this. The thing is, that I do feel somewhat responsible for his actions. I know that they were his actions and not mine, but I still feel terrible for what he put you two through. When I saw him in that hallway with his gun to your head; I had no doubt that he intended to shoot you, or at least he would have, when he realized that I was there for him, and not for you. He might have felt cornered and he would have taken you with him, Jack. I couldn't allow that. He made me do the unthinkable. To take the life of one of your children is the hardest thing to do in this world; to have to choose between your children. I know I made the right choice. A choice between my bad son and my good one, really isn't a choice at all. It still hurts like hell," he finished, and sat looking down at his hands.

He wiped at the tears welling in his eyes again, and then sat motionless for a moment, before slowly lifting his head to look at us. Vicki was searching my face for answers. I was still wondering if I had heard him right, or if I misunderstood what he had said. I was trying to process a coherent thought, but it was like walking in the fog, trying to find my way.

Finally, the fog cleared a bit, and I was able to make sense of what he was saying.

"So, you knew that my Grandma switched me and bad Jack at birth?" I asked.

"What? No. She didn't switch you. You called him bad Jack? Fitting I guess. He was after all bad, as bad as they come," Karl said.

"I'm not following you. She told me, that she switched the two of us at birth, because she recognized early on, that he was a bad seed. What did you mean, when you said that you had to choose, between your bad son and your good one?" I asked, waiting impatiently for a response.

Karl remained silent for an impossibly long time.

I looked over at Vicki and she mouthed: "What the..."

I shrugged in response to her question. Karl grimaced as if he were in pain. It looked as though there was some sort of internal struggle going on in his mind. Perhaps, it was his turn to try and find his way through the fog. Finally, he spoke; slowly at first, methodically, thinking between each word spoken, finding his way.

"I see it now. Yes; I believe that your Grandma was telling the truth. I did notice a difference in his behaviour when he was very young. I don't remember his exact age, your exact age, but I do remember now. I had forgotten about that, until just now," he said.

"You still didn't answer me. What did you mean, when you said that you had to choose?" I asked.

"I shouldn't have said that," he said.

"But you did!" I said.

"Okay. I know you've been through a lot, but I have too. I'll level with you. You are a grown man and you deserve to know the truth. We've come this far. I guess we've reached the point of no return, haven't we? I'm going to need another drink of liquid courage, in order to finish."

Vicki squeezed my hand. I knew what she was saying. "Whatever it is, we'll get through it together."

I wondered what could possibly be taking Bruce so long, but then again, I was glad that he had given us our space. This conversation wasn't going at all like I had expected.

Karl came back with his beer, sat it on the table, then pushed it away, unopened.

"You have to understand, I'm no home wrecker. I would never intentionally be with another man's wife. I don't want you to be upset with your Mother. Your Mother and Father were going through a tough time. She was scared, she was lonely, and she was miserable. I didn't know that they were still together, and I'm not so sure, that she thought that they were either. We met, and immediately we hit it off. She just wanted to be loved and appreciated, and I loved your Mother very much. I still do in fact. She was torn between a life with me, and one with your Father. A life with your Father looked hopeless at the time, but she took her wedding vows seriously, and eventually she decided to give her marriage every chance to succeed. I was devastated, but your Dad is a good man, and I understand her decision. They picked up the pieces and they seem to be very happy today. I ended up marrying shortly afterwards. I know it isn't right, it's unfair to my wife, but I've never been able to love her like I loved your Mother. I think my wife can feel it deep down. I feel terrible about that. I do love her, it's just not the same," he said, exhaling loudly.

He seemed emotionally spent, exhausted.

"I'm trying to make sense of this. I'll just say it out loud and you tell me if I've got it straight. A couple of weeks ago, I found out in a letter from my Grandma that I was switched at birth, with the other Jack from our sister world. Fast forward a couple of weeks. Now I find out that you are still my biological Father, so that part hasn't changed. The man that I thought was my Father, the whole time that I was growing up, is in fact not my real Dad, but my Mother is my real Mother again. Does that about cover it?"

"It would appear as though that's correct," he said.

"Are you okay, Jack?" Vicki whispered in my ear.

"I will be. I'm starting to get used to being out of my comfort zone. I'm starting to forget what my somewhat normal, safe life felt like. I'm just glad that you're here with me. That's what matters more than any of this," I said, and kissed her.

"I appreciate you telling me all of this. I can tell that it wasn't easy for you, and I can't imagine what you must be going through. Let's just take a break from all our worries. I know of no better way, than to spend some time with Bruce and his brothers. They have a way of making all my troubles go away, if only for a short while," I said.

We sat in awkward silence until Bruce returned with the beer. He borrowed a cart from the custodian to carry four cases of beer up the elevator and into his study hall.

"You really are expecting to let your hair down tonight, aren't you?" I said.

He set the cart down in the middle of the floor and flattened his hair with the palms of his hands, and then continued into his study. Vicki couldn't contain her laughter this time when his hair immediately started to stick up from his head again. She buried her head under my arm to hide her laughter.

He either didn't notice or chose to ignore it.

"I know what it's like when my brothers and I get together. You know," he said to me.

"I sure do. We're going to stick around for a while, if that's okay," I said.

"I'd have it no other way. I know the boys are dying to meet Vicki," Bruce said.

"I think I'm going to take off. It's been a long couple of days and the Missus needs me to be home right now. Besides, I'm not in the mood to be around other people I'm afraid... I think I need some quiet time, if you don't mind?" Karl said.

"I completely understand. Try to get some rest, take care of yourself. I'll catch up with you in a couple of days. If you need anything, give me a call," Bruce said.

"I will, thanks. Nice to have officially met you both. I hope that we can stay in touch," Karl said, tiredly.

Vicki stood up, gave him a long hug and whispered something in his ear. I stood as well and shook his hand.

"We will," I said.

That seemed to brighten his mood. "That's good, very good. I would say," he said, and we all laughed.

"Oh, I get it, make fun of the old guy. You'd miss me if I weren't here, I would say," Bruce said, and we all broke out in a fit of laughter.

"I'm guessing that your talk with Karl went reasonably well, under the circumstances?" he said, when Karl left.

"As well as could be expected I guess. I'm still holding on to the dream of having some sort of normal life someday," I said.

"That's good, very good..." Bruce started.

"I would say," Vicki and I said in perfect unison, and we all laughed again.

Bruce's brothers showed up and we all drank way more than we needed too, and of course, Vicki fell in love with them at once. Her reaction was much the same as mine, the first time that I met them. She never stopped laughing or smiling once, the entire evening; that I saw anyway.

It was so amazing to have her back in my life again. This was truly the happiest I had ever been. Not that there was ever any doubt that Vicki was the one for me, but I was sure now, more than I had ever been.

CHAPTER EIGHTEEN

The last couple of months were the most trying ones in my entire life, but it did serve to bring me and Vicki closer together. My Mom and Dad were always going to be my parents, but Vicki and I made a point of including Karl in our lives and I think that we were all better for it.

She gave up her lease on her apartment and never went back, except to pack her things. We were married the next year. Bruce and all his brothers were at the wedding. George brought his new girlfriend Kate who we have come to adore since. She has had a very positive affect on him and he will never again be known as Stinky. Helen, Jason and the kids are doing well, and we still get together regularly with them and my parents. Things are amazing in fact. We have such a wonderful circle of friends and family. I couldn't have asked for better.

It was a process to get to this point and it didn't happen over night. Most of my life I had either been bullied or been pre-occupied with bad Jack. I didn't know how big of a toll that it had taken on me. I thought that I had dealt with all those feelings and they were now in the past, but I couldn't have been further from the truth. Vicki helped as much as she could, but it took a year of therapy, once a week, before I finally came to terms with the damage that all the bullying had caused and how bad Jack fit into it all. I don't think that he could have become such a central character in my life, if I hadn't been bullied as a child.

Bad Jack... well, he still visits me, but usually Henry is there to scare him off. I still see Grandma in my dreams as well. Visits from Grandma and Henry are always welcome ones.

***

We had a fairy tale wedding. All our friends and family told us that marriage was going to be hard, that you have to work at it every single day. That may be true for some, but for us, it is as easy and natural as breathing.

We've been married for four years now and couldn't be happier. Today is our wedding anniversary, which also happens to be the twins' birthday.

Two years ago, today, Vicki gave birth, to beautiful twin girls. We named them Rachel and Raven and they are our pride and joy. Rachel has long blonde hair and is as sweet and caring as her Mother. Raven has long black hair and has an impulsive side that reminds me of Vicki when we first met.

You're probably wondering if the girls can jump from our world to our sister world. Not yet, which is a bit odd, considering they are twins, but I can see it in their eyes. The eyes can't lie.

Rachel and Raven are playing on the lawn. It's a beautiful spring day, perfect weather for this time of year. Vicki is sitting beside me holding my hand and watching the girls play. Everyone should be arriving soon for the girls' birthday party. Life couldn't possibly get any better.

Rachel looks back and waves at us with her little hand. We blow her kisses and she pretends to catch them.

Raven looks back at us, pushes her sister hard to the ground. She turns and waves at us, a twisted grin spreads across her tiny face.

She reaches above her head and rips open the blue sky. The terrible sound of ripping cardboard and broken glass breaks the stillness of the day. She walks through.

The world closes in around her, and she is gone.

THE END

AFTERWORD

Peripheral is the second book I wrote, followed by The Suffering. Chapter five in both books are roughly the same but they are told from different view points. In Peripheral we see it from Jack's point of view and in The Suffering, it is told from Billy's. The books are unrelated, but they do have the characters, Billy, Henry and Jack in common.

I had the idea for The Suffering and I needed a protagonist. Who better than Billy Johnson? I liked his character and his brother Henry as well, and I wasn't ready to say good bye, just yet.

Your first impression of someone, whether it's good or bad, is only that, a first impression. You don't know their back story, what made them the way they are and what brought them to that point in their lives. I felt it was unfair to Billy's character for him to be seen as one dimensional. He was so much more than a bully. It was important to me, to show the reader how Billy and Henry got to that bridge in the forest on that day and what made him who he was. I wanted to give him the depth of character that he deserved. It was the least I could do for one of my favourite inky friends.
Dan Mayer, May 20, 2019.

NOTE FROM THE AUTHOR

Word-of-mouth is crucial for any author to succeed. If you enjoyed the book, please leave a review online—anywhere you are able. Even if it's just a sentence or two. It would make all the difference and would be very much appreciated.

Thanks!
Dan

ABOUT THE AUTHOR

Delhi, Ontario-based Dan Mayer likes to talk, write and talk about his writing. He is an avid outdoors man, who fishes, hunts, travels, scuba dives, and rides a motorcycle. He has four grown children, two beagles and a red-fox lab. Working as a millwright funds his many adventures which fuel his imagination. Peripheral is his third published novel.